Undefeated

Scott Hildreth

Published by
Eralde Publishing

Cover Design Copyright © Creative Book Concepts
Text Copyright © Scott Hildreth
Formatting by Creative Book Concepts

ISBN 13: 978-0692325582

DEDICATION

This book is dedicated to every woman who has developed the courage to walk away from an abuser and into the arms of someone who appreciates and accepts her for who she is.

If this is you, hold your head high.

If you are in an abusive relationship, my recommendation is to get out now.

Because your Shane Dekkar is waiting.

PROLOGUE

"So this kid's going to be here by 3:00?" the trainer asked as he turned away from the boxing ring.

The manager of the gym nodded, providing his best form of assurance the boxer would arrive for the afternoon match.

"Where's he from again?" the trainer asked as he picked up some loose medical tape from the floor.

"Compton," the manager responded.

"As in Compton, California?" the trainer asked as he tossed the tape into the trash can beside the ring.

"That's what he said. Compton, California," the manager said as he walked toward the locker room.

The trainer walked alongside the manager as he rubbed two days growth of beard between his thumb and forefingers.

"White kid?" he asked.

The manager nodded.

"And you said he's *riding* here? As in he's riding a *motorcycle?*"

As they entered the locker room, the manager turned and nodded.

"What do you know about him? Just seems kinda weird. The kid says he's undefeated, and he's moving *here*, of all places. The fact he insisted on fighting the day he rides into town on a fucking motorcycle is just asking for getting his ass handed to him," the trainer stated as he sat on the bench in the middle of the room.

"It's just like I told you. He said he needed a trainer *and* a manager. Told me his grandfather died, and that he had been acting as both. Kid says he weighs about a hundred ninety, but carries two twenty real well. He sounds eager as hell. Shit, he's from southern California. There's fighters all over the place you and I never heard of - don't make 'em good or bad," the manager said as he sat on the bench beside the trainer.

Slowly, he looked around the locker room.

"It'd be kind of nice to have some fresh talent in here, that's for sure. Who you got set to fight him?" the trainer asked as he stared at the lockers which lined the wall in front of him.

The manager looked over his shoulder and smiled a slow smile, "Mike."

As his face filled with surprise, the trainer turned to face the manager, "Ripton? *The Ripper*?"

The manager nodded.

"Joe, that's going to be a one-sided affair don't you think?" the trainer chuckled as he shook his head from side-to-side.

"I suppose so," the manager laughed in return, "just figured as eager as this kid was, and the fact he said the word *undefeated* about ten times in our first conversation, I'd teach him a quick lesson about how we do it here in Texas. You can build him back up from there, Kelsey."

"So that's why Ripton's been here since lunch, ain't it?"

The manager turned his head and nodded.

"So what you thinking about this?" the manager asked as he turned and looked in the direction of the locker lined wall.

The trainer shrugged his shoulders as he slowly turned his head and stared at the lockers lining the wall. He looked at his watch and toward the lockers again. The manager glanced toward him and raised both eyebrows as he placed his hands on his knees and waited for a response. Now, with one eyebrow still raised, the manager stared at the wall and slowly narrowed his eyes.

"It's ten before," Kelsey said as he stared at the lockers.

"Well, personally, I think we ought to stick with blue. If we're going to make this place look like something, we ought to paint the *wall* a different color, not the lockers. Them steel lockers never hold paint very well. Blue. That's my opinion," Joe said as he stood up from the bench.

As the trainer smiled and stood from the bench, he turned his ear toward the wall, squinted his eyes, and looked down at the floor.

"You hear that?" Kelsey asked as the loud roar of an approaching motorcycle could be heard.

The manager nodded, "I suppose it's him, don't you?"

"Let's go sit in our seats and see what this kid's all about. And I'm fine with blue. I didn't mean to stare at it so damned long, but I ain't never been too good at color schemes. Let's try a light yellow or something calming on the walls," Kelsey said as he turned toward the door.

"*Calming.* I like that. Yellow it is," Joe agreed.

As the two men entered the gym, a young man came in through the front door. Dressed in a hooded sweat shirt, jeans and boots, he walked into the gym and took a deep breath as he looked around. When he noticed the two older men, he turned and began walking toward them. His walk had a certain swagger.

An expressed confidence.

Joe looked up and down the fighter's body as he spoke, "You the kid from Compton?"

"Yes sir. Shane Dekkar," the young man responded as he held his right hand out.

"Son of a bitch kid, you got a grip on you, kid. God damn. I'm Joe Murphy, we spoke on the phone," the manager acknowledged as he shook the young man's hand.

The young man turned to the trainer and held out his hand. Reluctantly, the trainer gripped his hand and offered a handshake in return.

"Kelsey O'Reilley. I'm the trainer who *might* train you. And it's kind of hot for a hooded sweatshirt ain't it?" the trainer asked as he shook the young man's hand.

"I'd sure appreciate it, sir. My grandfather was my trainer and my manager both. He passed unexpectedly. That's what brought me here. And you'll find I wear this hoodie year round, sir. Are we still on for three o'clock?" the young man asked as he adjusted his backpack.

The trainer shook his head as he looked at the young man. Two men sparred lightly in the ring behind them. The manager smiled as he looked from the ring toward the young man. The trainer looked down at his watch and grinned.

"You sure you want to do this, kid?" the manager asked.

The young man nodded his head once, "Yes sir."

"I only need ten minutes to change and warm up," he responded.

"Ten minutes?" the trainer coughed, "ten?"

The young man smiled and nodded, "Where's the locker room?"

"Follow me. It's not much to look at, but we're considering new paint," the trainer said as he began walking toward the locker room.

"So, you're undefeated?" the trainer turned and asked.

"Yes sir," the young man answered as he adjusted his back pack.

"Well, this ain't a title fight. All it's for is so we can see what you're about. If you are what you claim kind of deal. You understand, son?" he asked as they turned to the locker room.

The young man nodded his head once as he got undressed, "Yes sir. I understand. I just need to get a fight in. I haven't fought in two weeks."

"Two weeks. Hell, that's no kind of wait," the trainer said as he sat down on the bench.

The trainer looked up as the young man removed gear from his bag.

"It is for me, sir. I try to fight at least once a day, and I train five days a week," the young man responded.

"At that pace you'll burn out quick," the trainer responded as the young man pulled his shorts on.

"Sir, do you expect you'll train me?" the young man asked as he handed the trainer a roll of tape.

As the trainer looked the young man's hands over and began to tape them, he responded, "I *might*. We'll see how you do. This fella you're gonna fight will be a tough one for you. He's never been knocked down, never been knocked out, and never lost. We'll see how you look against him."

The young man looked intently into the eyes of the trainer and nodded once.

"Care to ask me what he weighs? Or his age? His fighting record?" the trainer asked.

"No sir," the young man responded.

The trainer shook his head at the perceived arrogance of the young man.

"God damn, you street fight much?" the trainer asked as he taped the heavily scarred hands of the young man.

The young man nodded once.

"Tattoo mean something?" the trainer asked as he noticed the tattooed knuckles of the man's right hand.

The young man nodded once, "Yes sir."

"Bust these hands up too much, and your career will end quickly, son," the trainer said softly as he inspected the young man's hands.

"Former military?" the trainer asked as he slid the gloves over the young man's freshly taped hands.

"No sir, they were my fathers," the young man responded, making reference to the dog tags that dangled on a chain from his neck.

The trainer looked the young man over.

"You're built like a brick shit house, kid. You lift weights?" he asked.

The young man nodded.

As the trainer laced the gloves, he nodded his head slowly.

"What are you going to do for warm up?" he asked.

"I pulled the bike over and ran three miles before I got here, I'm ready. Just need to get my head right, sir," the young man responded.

The trainer raised one eyebrow as he looked at the young man.

"I need to pray, sir. I'll be ready in a minute," the young man responded.

"Well, you can't wear those in the ring," the trainer said as he reached for the dog tags which hung from the young man's neck.

The young man immediately jerked his body to the right and raised his gloves in a defensive posture.

"Damn, son. I'm just going to pull 'em off and put 'em in the locker with your stuff," the trainer responded.

"I'll ask you to remove them before I step into the ring," the young man responded.

"Let's just toss 'em in here with your..."

"I'll ask you to remove them before I step into the ring," the young man repeated as he interrupted the trainer in mid-sentence.

"Alright. You do that," the trainer responded as he slipped the protective gear over the head of the young man.

"You need to pray?" the trainer asked as he put the bag, back pack, and clothes into a locker.

"I'm ready sir," the young man responded as he pounded his gloves together.

The trainer shook his head and started walking out of the locker room. The young man followed. The swagger of the young man was exaggerated in comparison to the slow steady shuffle of the elderly manager.

The young man stepped up into the ring and leaned toward the ropes. As he lowered his head he spoke to the trainer.

"Keep these in your hand, sir. Or put them in your pocket. Please don't set them down or wear them," he said.

The trainer reached into the ring and removed the dog tags from the young man's neck.

"So, kid's in the military?" the manager asked the trainer.

"Nope. Said they were his father's," the trainer responded as he put the dog tags in his pocket.

"Well, what are we gonna do here?" the manager asked.

"Hell, I don't know. Wanna have 'em go ten rounds?" the trainer asked.

The manager nodded.

"Mike!" the manager screamed across the gym.

A very muscular man in his early thirties walked slowly toward the group, stepped under the ropes and into the ring. As he entered in the ring, he stood on his toes and stretched his calves. His body tan, his head cleanly shaven, and his upper torso and arms covered with tattoos, he began to rock back and forth on the balls of his feet as he stared toward the young man. The man looked extremely intimidating as he pounded his gloves together.

The trainer stepped into the ring.

The two men approached one another.

"Fellas, this ain't for nothing but bragging rights. Both of you are undefeated. Should be a good little sparring match. Mike, this kid just rode a bike here from California. Hasn't really warmed up," the trainer took a breath.

"I'm ready, sir," the young man responded.

"Mike, this is Shane Dekkar. Shane this is Mike Ripton," the trainer said.

The two men nodded at each other and touched gloves. The bald headed man stared into the eyes of the young man and winked.

"Alright, you two know how this works. I suppose we'll go ten," the trainer said.

The two men nodded and separated. Mike Ripton walked slowly to the corner of the ring.

The young man followed the trainer to the opposite corner. The trainer inserted a mouthpiece into the young man's mouth.

"You sure you're ready?" the trainer asked.

The young man nodded as he bit down on his mouth piece.

"At the bell," the trainer stated.

The young man nodded.

The trainer positioned himself beside the manager of the gym and sat down at the table beside the boxing ring. As the two men sat at the table, the young man pounded his gloves together and growled.

"Well, let's see what this kid's got. Is he fucking growling?" the manager asked the trainer quietly.

The trainer smiled and nodded his head, "Sure sounds like it."

Ding!

The two fighters approached each other cautiously. The young man took a stance with his right foot forward and began to study the other fighter. A few flurries of punches to the young man's body followed.

"Southpaw?" the trainer asked.

The manager shrugged his shoulders.

The young man switched his feet to an orthodox stance, now leading with the left foot.

"What's he doing?" the trainer asked.

The manager shrugged his shoulders again.

The young man unleashed several punches to the lower torso of the other fighter.

"God damn, he's quick," the manager stated as he stood and crossed his arms.

The young man threw a quick right jab, sending the other fighter backward.

"Shit, he's got the Ripper on his heels," the trainer said as he stood from the bench.

The young man followed with a left jab, and a quick right hook. Ripton stepped backward and attempted to become stable on his feet. His feet staggered as he stepped. As the young man leaned toward the body of Ripton, he swung a devastating left uppercut.

The glove made a crushing impact with Ripton's chin.

"God damn, this kid's….*oh, shit*. Ripper's *down*," the trainer said as Mike Ripton fell to the mat.

The young man stepped to the side of Ripton's body.

Ripton's trainer jumped into the ring and ran toward his motionless body. As Ripton's trainer spoke, he slowly raised himself to his elbows.

Ripton's trainer waved his arms toward Kelsey, indicating that the fight was over.

"Looks like you got a new fighter, huh Kelsey?" the manager chuckled lightly.

"Looks like it," the trainer responded.

"Come here, kid," the trainer said sternly toward the young man.

"*Come here*," the trainer repeated as he held the ropes upward.

The young man, focused on the body in the center of the ring, shook his head from side-to-side.

Slowly, Mike Ripton sat up. As he stood, for stability, he held onto the shoulder of his trainer. As Ripton began to move, the young man slowly walked to the center of the ring.

The young man tapped his glove on the shoulder of the other fighter.

"Good fight," the young man said.

"Nice shot, kid. I didn't even see that fucker coming," Ripton said over his shoulder.

The young man turned and walked slowly toward the trainer.

The trainer held the ropes upward as the young man stepped under them and out of the ring.

"Are you interested in working with me?" the young man asked.

"Kelsey, call me Kelsey. And the answer is yes, kid," the trainer responded.

"Shane Dekkar, sir. That's my name. I'd prefer it if you call me

Shame On, Shame, Shane, Dekkar, or Dekk, sir. I don't particularly like being called *kid*," the boxer stated.

The manager chuckled as the boxer chastised the trainer.

"Well, *Shane*. Welcome to Austin, Texas," the trainer responded as he pulled the boxer's dog tags from his pocket.

The boxer stepped from beside the ring, bent at the waist, and lowered his head toward the trainer's hands. The trainer reached over the boxer's head and placed the dog tags around his neck and removed his headgear.

"I'm going to change and go see the city. If possible, sir, have me a fight for tomorrow afternoon," the boxer said.

"Call me Kelsey, *I don't particularly like being called sir*," the trainer smiled as he responded.

"Noted," the boxer said as he nodded his head once sharply.

The boxer turned and began walking toward the locker room. His walk possessed a certain confidence – a swagger.

"Why you suppose he walks like that?" the manager asked as he watched the boxer walk away.

"*Because he can*," the trainer responded.

KACE

Trying to figure a way to get out of a relationship and not feel like a complete failure was difficult. Most people would never understand why I stayed in the situation with Josh as long as I had. As much as I hated the way had treated me, giving up on our relationship was never an option.

I couldn't fathom being alone.

When I thought of it, my head got all jumbled up and I became scared.

Sometimes when I considered leaving him I began to shake. As soon as it happened, I would change my mind. I often wish someone would simply be able to decide for me.

Each time he had beaten me, I deserved it. When I was eighteen, Josh was twenty-one. I recall one evening he had to work overtime, and he came home exhausted from a long day at work. He immediately asked me about dinner, and I back talked him. He quickly lost his temper. He never would have hit me if I hadn't talked back.

It was a really long day for him, and I should have known better.

Each time he hit me, he later reminded me it never would have happened if I didn't deserve it. He always told me he wished he didn't *have* to do it. He explained if I would just learn to respect him, he wouldn't have to hit me. Sometimes I wish I *would* learn my lesson. Other times I wish I was with someone else; someone who didn't have to hit me to teach me things.

Josh and I met when I was sixteen. I had never been intimate with anyone else or even talked to another man for that matter. Josh didn't let me talk to other men, and he monitored my text messages and phone calls. He forbid me from having Instagram, Snapchat, Facebook or Twitter. He often took my cell phone and checked through all of the files whenever he wanted to, looking for pictures. He explained how it taught me to be honest and loyal. I imagined he was right, but it still bothered me.

While working, I often read on my break. I daydream what it would be like to have a man treat me the way the women are treated in the books I read. I doubted those types of men really actually existed. If they did, I'd love to have a man like that. It would be nice to feel wanted.

Josh had not had sex with me for several years and I began to feel ugly as a result. A woman needs to feel wanted. Even if she didn't feel loved, she should feel as if someone desired her.

Because Josh didn't make me feel loved at all, and had not for years, I often daydreamed about other men. I would never cheat on Josh, and even though he wasn't nice to me, all I wanted was for him to simply want me. I consistently wished he desired something I had to offer him.

His desire, however, never came. I never daydreamed about a man saving me. I wasn't like those girls in the books.

I didn't need to be *saved*.

I chose to be in my relationship with Josh because I wanted it to eventually work, and I didn't want to give up on us or look at myself as a failure. I only wanted to be loved. I'm a strong woman, and my persistence stands as proof of my strength. I simply needed to find a way to be strong enough to make our relationship last until he loved me.

Recently, I had begun to think about the stories I often read about. To have the hardship, the recovery, and the lasting relationship which always came in the end was something which appealed to me. It really started when Josh held his knife to my throat and told me I was a dumb bitch. On that particular night we had been arguing more than normal because he quit making love to me.

The first time I asked why, he slapped me and said it was because he wasn't attracted to me any longer. He said I was ugly inside and out. He never slapped me once whenever he chose to slap me. He slapped me until he was tired of slapping me, or until I *learned my lesson.*

The second time I asked about wanting him to make love to me, he choked me and held me against the wall by my throat. I blacked out and later woke up on the floor.

The third time I asked, he held his knife to my throat and told me to never ask again. Josh had a temper, and I didn't want to learn any kind of lesson that has to do with a knife. I just wanted him to love me the way I loved him.

I tried, and I tried, and I tried, but I couldn't seem to ever make the right decisions with Josh. I had continuously made bad choices which eventually make him mad. I wished just once he would be happy with me, and maybe tell me he liked what I cooked him for dinner.

I always tried so hard.

He used to tell me those things, but not anymore.

I had been excited all week to watch a movie with him. Josh told me if I didn't do anything stupid all week, he would rent a movie on Friday and we would try to watch it together. I thought maybe it will be the night things turned around for the better. *If we could get along for just one night, I would hold on to those memories forever.*

As I sat in the truck with my Kindle, Josh got out and walked toward the Red Box to get the movies. I sat quietly and read quickly as Josh looked through the selection of the available movies. Reading had become my form of escaping. It allowed me freedom from everything by living through the stories I read. It was easy for me to dream of being the female character in the books I read. A good book could make me laugh, cry, or get so aroused I had to touch myself. Without reading, I would go completely insane.

My Kindle had become my savior.

"They ain't got *Black Hawk Down* or *Pulp Fiction*," he said over his shoulder as he stood in front of the Red Box, staring at the screen.

We had not watched too many movies over the ten years we had been together, but we had seen those two movies no less than a dozen times a piece. I liked doing almost anything with Josh, but sometimes I wish he would think about me and my desires. I'd like to watch *The Notebook* or something similar. Maybe *Safehaven*.

"Well, fuck. They ain't got nothin' to watch at this shit-hole. Fuckin' pisses me off. Maybe we should just hit the liquor store and get a thirty pack and hang out at the house," he said as he got into the truck.

I slipped the Kindle into my purse. My heart sank as he started the truck. Josh drank a lot. When he drank, it made me nervous. When he was drunk, he was always mean. He felt he *deserved* to drink; because I either drove him crazy or he had a tough day at work. I tried to hide from him when he drank, but hiding tonight would be impossible to do.

"Why you got that shitty look on your face?" he muttered as he

16

shoved his lip full of tobacco.

I shook my head slowly.

"What? You got something to say? I really ain't in the mood for your mouth, you little bitch," he barked as he wiped his hand on his jeans.

I wanted to tell him to get a different movie. I felt like crying. Why couldn't we have a night together and *not* fight? Why did he have to drink so much? Why did he have to chew tobacco? It made his breath stink and his teeth brown. To have him be kind to me for one night, I'd let him beat me for a week.

A week of having my face slapped and called names.

In exchange for one night of calling me beautiful and kissing me.

"I asked you a fucking question," his jaw tightened as he shut off the truck.

Oh no. Not here. Please not here. Please, Josh.

"You see what I mean? You fuckin' *ask* for it. It's like you *want* it. I'll never understand what drives you to fight with me, woman," he yelled.

My muscles tensed as he opened the truck door and stepped out and into the parking lot. He slowly walked around in front of the truck and around to my door. After glaring in the window at me, he opened it.

"Gimme your fuckin' purse," he snarled as he held his hand out toward me.

"Gimme that sum bitch or I'll slap your mouthy little ass right here in the parking lot," he growled through his clenched teeth as he spit tobacco juice into the parking lot by his feet.

I handed him my purse.

He opened my purse and looked inside. He reached into it, shuffled through the contents, and pulled out my Kindle.

"This little motherfucker's become a problem. I know you talk to people on it. I *know* you do. Talk to people and read that fuckin' filth," he tossed it onto the asphalt beside his feet.

"Josh, no. Please," I begged.

"What, afraid you ain't gonna be able to reach your fuckin' boyfriend? You little whore," he snapped as he raised his boot over the Kindle.

I covered my eyes as he held his boot over the Kindle. I couldn't stand to watch whatever he was going to do.

"Josh, no. I don't have a boyfriend. And I don't talk to people with it. It's a Kindle. I just use it to read. It's my only way to escape," I sobbed as I moved my hands from my eyes.

"Escape? What the fuck you gotta escape from? See? You always dig a hole," he held his boot over the Kindle, raised his eyebrows, and spit again.

"It's that mouth Kace. It's always getting' you in trouble. See? Now I *gotta* do this, and it's your fault. You did it, not me," he said as he stomped the screen of the Kindle with his boot.

As he twisted his heel into the shattered screen he shook his head.

"I *was* gonna scare ya and give it back. But hell no, you had to pop off and get lippy. Hell, I'd have liked to had a good night and a fuckin' movie together. You just don't seem to give a fuck about my *feelings*, Kace," he said as he bent down to pick up the smashed Kindle.

I looked down and wiped the tears from my face.

"Everything alright?" an unfamiliar voice asked from my right side.

I wiped my face and looked up through the opened truck door.

Ohmygod.

And there he stood.

In faded jeans, black boots, dark hair, sunglasses, and a black hoodie

18

he stood outside the truck door. He had his hands in his hoodie pockets and the hood half over his head. He quickly alternated glances between Josh and I. Slowly he pulled his hand from his pockets and removed his sunglasses. As he turned my direction his steel grey eyes met mine and he paused. I wanted him to help me. Save me from Josh and take me away.

But.

I said nothing. I only stared.

His face was covered in a few days growth of beard. He was absolutely gorgeous. His jaw was tight and his facial features distinct. And. Those. Eyes.

"Ain't nobody talkin' to you, slick," Josh said.

Slowly and methodically, the stranger turned from facing me to face Josh.

"Well, I was addressing both of you, asshole. But I suppose now I'm speaking to *her*. Are you alright?" his tone changed from stern to pleasant and soft as he turned from Josh to face me again.

He studied my face. Although his mouth didn't form one, his eyes smiled. The temperature in the truck rose a hundred degrees. I melted into my seat. He was absolutely gorgeous, just like I imagined my book boyfriends.

Take me with you, please. Save me.

I nodded.

"Are you sure?" he asked softly.

"Kace," Josh said flatly.

Quickly, he turned and looked at Josh. As he stood and stared, waiting for Josh to speak, Josh looked down at the ground and remained quiet. The stranger slowly turned back toward me.

I nodded.

The stranger turned to Josh, who was holding the smashed Kindle in his hand.

"Ain't your business, slick," Josh said as he slowly looked up from the ground.

"Well, as I was getting off my bike, I heard the word *whore*. I looked up and watched you stomping on *that*," the stranger said as he pointed to my smashed Kindle.

"I don't let men abuse women in my presence. So, it is kind of my business. And my name isn't slick, asshole," the stranger said angrily.

"We just had a disagreement. Ain't nobody getting' abused here," Josh said softly as he looked down at the surface of the parking lot.

"Well, I suppose as long as you're done being an asshole, and she's okay," the stranger paused and looked into the truck.

"It's *no longer* my business," the stranger said as he walked around Josh slowly. His stride was unique. He had a certain way of walking that made him very intriguing.

His steel grey eyes never left Josh.

"Well, she was bein' disrespectful. We got in a pissin' match. Like I said, ain't nothin' to do with you," Josh said to the stranger as he slowly walked around the truck.

As Josh opened the door to the truck, the stranger leaned onto the edge of the Red Box and focused on me. As he waited for us to back up, he put his sunglasses back on. His right hand had tattooed knuckles.

Squeeeeee!

Josh tossed the crushed Kindle at me as he got in the truck.

"What the fuck you lookin' at? And why the fuck is he starin' at you?" Josh asked as he started the truck.

As I admired the stranger, I was speechless. I shrugged my shoulders.

"Fuckin'asshole. I shoulda punched his ass," Josh snarled as he began to back the truck out of the parking spot.

I would have loved to see you try that.

As he put the truck in gear and started pulling forward, I looked out the window at the stranger and silently mouthed the words…

Help me.

SHANE

Two weeks. That's all it took. Two fucking weeks.

Come on, shut your mouth. Don't go there. Please, mister, don't do it. Not now, I'm trying to eat. Just be cool.

I pressed the hoodie to the sides of my face.

Just shut your mouth dude.

"If you don't learn how to act in public, I'll teach you. You ain't gonna like it, though," he said as he took another drink of his beer.

I sliced my chicken and took another bite. Chicken and turkey seemed to keep me in good health, and I made it a point to find the best places to eat both. In the two weeks that I'd been in Austin, this restaurant had proven to have some of the best grilled chicken I had ever eaten. I had a sinking feeling, however, they wouldn't allowed me to return after tonight. At least not without being questioned.

"I try and act the best I know how to. You're never satisfied," she responded from the other side of the table.

"Never satisfied? You dumb cunt. Never satisfied? I'm gonna slap some sense into you when we get home," he said as he pushed his plate to the center of the table.

Well, that could be a figure of speech. Not one I like. But this isn't my business.

"Paul. Please. I'm sorry, don't hit me again," she whispered.

Well, fuck. It just became my business.

I stood up, popped my neck, and pulled out my wallet. I removed a fifty dollar bill and placed it on the table. It was the least I could do for the ten dollar piece of chicken. This could get ugly real quick, and I didn't want to take advantage of the waitress.

Forgive me Lord for what I am about to do.

I walked across the floor to the table where the couple was sitting. I wiped my hands on my jeans and cracked my knuckles.

"Paul, I really need to talk to you," I said softly.

"How the fuck you know my name?" he asked as he looked up from his beer.

Well, she just said your name, you idiot. The entire restaurant knows.

"You don't remember me?" I lied.

He narrowed his gaze and shook his head, "Nope."

"Well, we need to talk," I said quietly, "Let's take a quick walk, this shouldn't take long."

"Paul, what's this about," she asked.

"Shut up, bitch. I have no idea who this weirdo is," he responded as he looked across the table toward her.

I really hoped this could have gone easier.

Maybe I should have left a hundred bucks.

Oh well...

I reached for his shoulder. As soon as my hand touched him, he came up with the beer bottle in his right hand. With the bottle cupped in his hand, he swung toward my face as he stood. I blocked his swing with my left arm and immediately punched him with two short right jabs. As he stumbled, I hit him once in the stomach with a surprise left hook. As he began to cough and sputter, I took the beer bottle from his hand and set it on the table.

Gasping for air and trying to catch his breath, he placed his hands on his knees.

"He may or may not be back in a minute," I said as I grabbed the man by his hair.

"Don't ever let this man beat you again, ma'am," I said to the woman as I began to pull him by his shirt and hair toward the door.

I figured I had ten minutes before the cops would show up. For me to make my point should take three.

As I drug him toward the door, he began to kick his feet and scream.

"Who the fuck do you think you are? You miserable son-of-a-bitch! Let me go," he yelled as I drug him through the front door and out to the concrete sidewalk beside the entrance to the restaurant.

Quickly, I reached for his back pocket and removed his wallet. As I searched for his driver's license, I held onto his hair tightly with my free hand. After finding it, I shoved his wallet in his shirt pocket and waved the license in front of his face.

"What the…" he began to say.

"Shut up," I interrupted.

I stuck his driver's license in the front pocket of my jeans.

"I'm on a time crunch so I'll make this quick. I overheard you telling your lady friend you were going to slap her when you got home. You're not going to slap her again, ever. I have your driver's license, so I know who you are and I know where you live. Here in about a week I'm going to come check on her, and if I find out you've touched her, I'm going to beat you worse than the beating you get tonight," I explained as I unzipped my hoodie.

As I pulled my hoodie over my shoulders, he took a swing.

The punch went by my face. I dropped my hoodie to the side and grabbed the hair on either side of his head. Immediately and with tremendous force, I thrust the top of my head into his face. I felt his nose crush under the impact.

As I released his hair from my grasp, I swung a fairly strong uppercut toward his chin. The punch connected to his jaw, knocked his teeth together, and lifted him from his feet. Unconscious, he immediately fell into a pile on the sidewalk.

You should hold your jaw tighter when you're in a fight, Paul.
Boxing 101.

I looked down at his motionless body and shook my head. I reached down and got my hoodie from the sidewalk, pulled it over my shoulders, and zipped it up. I stood over him as people watched and waited for him to become conscious.

As soon as he began to moan, I walked to my bike and fired it up.

Well, Paul, see you in a few weeks.

SHANE

If it is worth doing, it is worth doing right. Be the best you can be at whatever it is you choose to do. Sweeping the floor or washing the car. Nothing should ever be done half assed. I strived to be the best at anything and everything I ever decide to conquer.

Ever.

If I had attempting it and I did not succeed, you could believe I gave it my best effort, regardless of the outcome.

I choose to do very little, and be exceptional at what it is I decide to do. I would much rather be perceived as being great at a few things than be a failure at many. I have always been honest with myself and conscious of *who* I am, but that doesn't always help me understand *why* I am the way I am.

On the outside, I am always kind, polite, and considerate of others. On the inside, a beast resides. I don't know why or what fuels the demons inside of me, but I am very aware of their existence. My consciousness of their need, necessity, and deep desire to be fed is what has caused me to choose boxing as my main outlet.

I keep the demons fed, and they allow me to live an otherwise peaceful life. Fulfilling their hunger allows my desire to live a life of tranquility outside the boxing ring. As long as I continue to fight, they're fed. When they are fed, I am allowed.

Allowed to live.

I have been training in one way, shape or form since I was eleven. From what my trainers have always told me, I have tremendous stamina. I can train, fight, or work out for hours on end without becoming exhausted. For this I am grateful.

I have never been in a fight that I didn't feel was necessary. In the ring, people agree to fight me, knowing of my ability and my undefeated record. Boxing is a sport, and nothing more than a contest between two men – a contest of strength, stamina, willingness, and raw talent.

I have been in more street fights than I can count. Each time, I gave my opponent the ability to walk away. If they chose not to, I did what I had to do. In the ring or out, I have always stood the victor. The majority of my street fights were a result of me attempting to stand up for what I believed to be *morally* right.

I have never been afraid to fight for someone who can't stand up on their own, and there's not a shortage of people who act in a manner contrary to what I believe to be moral. Line every one of them up – every single one who abuses a woman, child, or the elderly and I'll beat them senseless one person at a time.

"So, what did you decide? Did you buy them?" Mike asked.

"No. I'm going to wait until the price goes down to something more affordable," I answered as I set my sandwich back onto the plate.

I wiped some mayonnaise from my mouth with my napkin and looked down at my boots.

"Dude, those fuckers are raggedy. Shit, I can see your socks through the bottom of the sole," he laughed.

"Yeah, but a hundred thirty bucks is a hundred thirty bucks," I shrugged my shoulders as I picked the sandwich up.

"You're one weird motherfucker, Dekkar. One weird motherfucker," he shook his head and laughed.

Mike was my first fight when I arrived in Austin two years prior. Even though I knocked him out for the first time in his career, we had become the best of friends, and never discussed that particular fight with others. I had no desire to be disrespectful to him or to his talent as a boxer.

Any man, on any given day, can be beaten by any other man. When the time comes, I will be beaten. Until then, I will remain grateful for my successes.

"Why do you have to go and say that, Ripp?" I mumbled, my mouth half full of sandwich.

"There are only a handful of people here that *know* you, because you're a fucking hermit. But I do, remember? Your father, no disrespect, died in Afghanistan. Your grandfather died two years ago – right before you came here. You inherited everything from *both* of them. I don't have any idea how much it was, but your father was a year from military retirement. Your grandfather *was* retired. I'm just going to guess you have a hundred and thirty bucks for a new pair of boots," he said over the top of his beer bottle as he drank the remaining portion in the bottle.

"Well, I hate to pay a hundred thirty if they're gonna go on sale for a hundred - or maybe ninety. Shit, that'd buy me a lot of turkey sandwiches," I responded, smiling.

"I'll have one more Ultra," Mike said to the waitress as he held his index finger in the air.

"You need anything, Dekk?" he asked, tilting his head back slightly.

"Water, please. Thank you, ma'am," I responded.

From the perspective of an outsider, Mike looked rather intimidating. He was a little taller than six feet, and weighed two hundred ten pounds. His head was shaved and he had tattoos on his upper arms, back and chest. His body was constructed entirely of muscle. Maintaining a perfect body and having an actual life outside of training is almost impossible. Some fighters have flab or fat on certain places. Mike wasn't one of those fighters. He trained and he trained hard. It was one reason we had become such close friends. He had my level of desire to maintain a healthy body and mind.

"*Water, please. Thank you, ma'am,*" Mike joked as the waitress walked away.

"You're so fucking proper and polite to women - and men - as long as they're *old* men. But you clench your jaw and look like a mean prick to everyone else. You crack me up, dude," he shook his head.

"Well, you look like a mean prick *all the time*," I smiled as I picked up the pickle from my plate.

Mike smiled an exaggerated smile, exposing his single gold tooth.

"That tooth is ridiculous. I'll never understand that," I said as I slid my plate to the side of the table.

"I told you already," he responded, still smiling.

"Yeah, I know. But it's horrid. Who wants to draw attention to the fact that they lost a tooth?" I said as I pulled my hood over my head.

"Well, I have a gold tooth, and you wear a fucking black hoodie everywhere you go. And in hot as hell Austin, Texas of all places. So, tell me more about this girl," he said as he picked at his teeth with a toothpick.

"There's nothing more to tell. I think she was a receptionist. I saw her sitting at a desk when I went to pay my insurance on the bike. That was the second time. I know I saw her two years ago at a drug store. This time, she didn't see me, I noticed her as I walked past her office. I got a bad feeling about the day in the parking lot of the drug store. I remember it specifically now. I'd kind of forgot about it," I pulled my hood tight around my head and peered through the hole.

"You know you do that, right?" he said as he pointed at my head.

"What?" I asked.

"You hide in your hood. When there's something you don't like talking about or doing," he answered.

I pulled the hood off of my head and ran my fingers through my hair as he started to speak again.

"Well, you quit talking when the waitress brought our food. What didn't you like? No, start by reminding me what bothered you about the first time you met her? You were talkin' and stopped, sorry," he said as he leaned onto the table.

Short of my grandfather, Mike was the best friend I have ever had. He truly cared about me as a person, and wasn't afraid to admit it. Since my first week here we had become extremely close and almost inseparable.

"She was sitting at a desk. Up the hallway at the building my insurance company is in. It might have been a law office, hell I don't know," I responded as I pulled my hood onto my head again.

"Whatever, that's boring. Tell me about the first time?" he asked as he leaned his forearms onto the edge of the table.

"Here you go. Anything else you two?" the waitress asked as she set the glass of water and the bottle of beer onto the table.

Mike looked up and shook his head, "Thanks."

He turned back toward me and waited.

"It was right when I got to town. And the guy she was with - I'm guessing her boyfriend - he was a douchebag. More like a *dirt* bag," I paused as I grabbed my glass of water.

"I was on the bike," I chuckled and shook my head as I remembered the evening.

"I was sitting on the bike looking at the soles of my boots. I heard him scream the word slut or whore, I don't remember. I looked up and he tossed and iPad or something on the ground. He screamed at her a few more times as I started walking over to his truck. Then he stomped the iPad and held it in his hand as he started yelling at her again."

"Surprised you didn't whip his ass," Mike said as he leaned back into his chair.

"Well, you know I struggle with that. If he had been violent toward her or threatening her I would have. They were just arguing. But when they left, she looked at me through the window. And her lips moved," I looked back up at the ceiling and studied the structure.

"Her *lips* moved?" he turned his palms up and looked at me surprised.

"Well, she either said *help me* or *hurt me* or something. I couldn't tell," I shook my head as I pressed my hood tight to my head with the palms of my hands.

"I kind of forgot about it until I went into the insurance company. Now I can't stop thinking about her. You believe there's a plan for all of us? You know, everything happens for a reason?" I asked.

"Yeah. I do. Kinda weird about that, but yeah," he said as he nodded his head slowly.

"I think things happen for a reason. I really do," I confirmed as I recalled seeing her sitting at the desk.

"What's she look like?" he asked.

I thought of the day at the drug store parking lot. She looked beautiful, but she was scared. I didn't like thinking about it. When I recalled the image of her talking on the phone as she sat at the desk, her blonde hair curly and shiny, I smiled. She looked magnificent.

"Perfect," I responded, still looking up at the lights.

"Oh, I gotcha. *Perfect*. If she robs a bank, we could give that description to the cops, Dekk. Did you see who robbed the bank? Yes, officer, I got a good look at her. Great. Can you describe her to the sketch artist? Yes, I sure can. *She looked perfect, officer*," he laughed as he tipped his beer bottle to his lips.

"Ripp, you're a prick. She's probably five foot *something*. She was in the truck, but looked short. Maybe a hundred pounds. Thin, but she looked athletic. So she's blonde and gorgeous," I looked down and focused on Mike's face as I finished speaking.

"What about *him*?"

"He was maybe six foot or so. Two twenty. Out of shape, but a big fucker," I rubbed my hood with my hands.

"Shitty brown hair, curly," I paused and thought for a second.

"Shitty beard. Shitty attitude. Just a shitty fucker," I grinned.

"Well, next time you go pay your insurance, if she's in there talk to her. Ask her about the day at the drug store. Give her a chance to say if she's even still with that guy," he responded as he raised his beer and tipped the mouth of the bottle my direction.

"You about ready to get out of here?" he asked as he lowered the empty bottle down onto the table.

I shrugged my shoulders and pushed my hands into the pockets of my hoodie.

"To where?" I asked.

"To the mall, Dekkar. I'm gonna help buy my buddy some boots," he said as he stood up and looked at the bill.

I pulled my hand from my pocket and reached for my wallet.

"I got this," he said as he waved his hands over the receipt the waitress had placed on the table.

"Times are tough and you need to save up for some boots," he laughed as he set the empty beer bottle down on top of the money and the receipt.

"Well, at least I don't ride in *those*," I said as I pointed to his shorts and Chuck's sneakers.

"Hell Shane, ask the waitress. Shit, ask anyone at the mall or on the way. Ask somebody at a fucking stoplight. Which one of us looks out of place? The one in the shorts and Chuck's or the guy wearing a fucking black hoodie when it's ninety degrees outside?" he laughed as he stuck his signature toothpick in his mouth.

I shook my head and walked toward the exit.

"I know, they're your security blankets. Your hoodie and those damned dog tags. Hell, Dekk. If it works, it works," he said as he slapped my shoulder.

I pulled my hand from my pocket and reached under my hoodie toward my chest.

Still there.

We walked out the door and directly to the bike parking, which was immediately outside the front door.

As I got on my bike, I began to think.

"Dude, you fall asleep?" Mike yelled over the sound of his rumbling exhaust.

"What?" I asked.

"You're in a fog, Dekk. You alright?" he asked.

I nodded.

"I was thinking," I responded as I grabbed the handlebars.

"About?" he asked.

"Upgrading the insurance on this bike," I responded.

KACE

I sat at my desk, waiting for my ten o'clock break. I loved taking my breaks because I could always read without feeling guilty. I had purchased a new Kindle, and had it shipped to my work office so Josh wouldn't know I had it. Trying to keep things from him made me feel like I was cheating, but he forced me to do most of the things I eventually chose to do.

He monitored all of my spending on the debit or credit cards, leaving me no real option to use the cards for anything but gas. I told him I ate out for lunch, and he provided me money to do so. Most days I would bring something light from home to eat. If I brought too much food, he'd notice and complain, so I brought very little when I did.

Most of the time, I would place my lunch money in my desk and save it for things I wanted or needed. Once I saved for a new pair of shoes. Recently, I bought the Kindle. I always went to the store and bought a prepaid debit card and used the card for the purchases. As long as I used the card, he never knew what I purchased and there was no record of it. For now I was leaving the Kindle in my desk so he couldn't take it and smash it.

I preferred reading romance and erotica. After I finished a really dark erotica, I would always follow it up with a true love romance novel. I had read some pretty dark erotica, and I actually liked reading them. I suspect I liked them because when I read about all of the crazy twisted dark stuff in those books it made my life seem almost normal.

I wished one of my book boyfriends would come and save me from my shit life I was living. Sometimes I thought I actually fell in love with the characters in the books and hated for the book, series, or story to end. I often found myself reading slower because I didn't want the book to end. I would daydream about the characters in the book, and what life would be like to have them instead of Josh.

When I remember the day we went to pick up a movie at the Redbox and Josh stomped my Kindle, it makes me sad. The man in the hoodie with the strange blue eyes – I think about him being a book boyfriend from time to time. I wish he would have saved me. I liked the way he walked. Austin is a huge city and I know I will never see him again, but I wish I could. I regret not saying something to him when he asked. He almost begged me to say something. And he called Josh an asshole twice. I liked that. I wanted to wrap my arms around him and tell him thank you.

I looked at my watch and realized it was 10:15 already. I spent most of my break daydreaming about the guy in the hoodie and not reading. Either way, it's was a means for me to escape. Josh told me no other man would ever want me and I am sure he is right. I put my Kindle back into my purse and walked to my desk.

"Kace, did the Valentine Group call or send you an email?" Mr. Martin asked as I sat down at my desk.

"Yes, they emailed and called both. I put together a spreadsheet based on last year's totals and incorporated the anticipated increases for this year's production costs. I made columns of each; projected profits are on the far right. I emailed it to you," I smiled.

"Kace, you amaze me. I don't know what I'd do without you," he slapped the desk and turned toward his office.

I liked it when Mr. Martin told me nice things, and he never hesitated to do so. He made me feel like I was not such a worthless person. He promoted me every few years, and gave me a big raise and a new title, but my work was always the same. My new title was Executive Secretary. I was the *only* secretary, but I liked the title.

Mr. Martin was in his early sixties and married. His wife came in from time to time, and she was beautiful. I would like to look like her when I'm sixty. I always told myself she looked so good because she was confident. Her hair, clothes, and nails were always perfect.

I know I am not supposed to be envious of anyone, but I envy her.

She has a nice husband, nice kids, a nice car, and a nice home. Her life couldn't get any better. I would settle to live in a shack with someone as long as they treated me nicely. I always thought Josh and I would get married and have children, but it never happened. Most of the time I was glad we never had kids.

I turned the music up on my computer. As *Jaymay's Grey or Blue* played, I slumped into my seat. I closed my eyes and relaxed to the music as it played. Getting lost in music was like getting lost in a book. I listened to the music, quite satisfied the Valentine Group had already called.

"*Grey or Blue*, great song," a voice said from in front of my desk.

I opened my eyes.

Holyfuckingshit.

I jumped forward so quickly I knocked over my bottle of water.

It was *him.*

39

"I didn't mean to startle you, were you asleep?" he asked softly.

"No. No. Sleeping not. Sleeping. Music. Listening. I was listening to music," I stammered.

Are you fucking kidding? I really don't want to stutter right now.

When I got excitedly nervous sometimes the words came out of my mouth and they were not necessarily always in order. I believe my mind worked at some weird pace, and often it got things jumbled up inside. I always tried to think before I spoke, but the words just fell out sometimes. And they always fell out in whatever order they wanted to.

It never happened when I was scared, only when I was really nervous and excited at the same time. It used to happen when I was a little girl on Christmas morning or on my birthday when I was young. When I first met Josh it would happen, because I used to be really excited to see him.

"Are you okay?" he asked softly.

As he spoke, he pulled his hood over his head. He wore the same black hoodie he had on at the Red Box when I saw him two years before. It seemed odd he was wearing a hoodie in the summer, but considering everything else, it really didn't matter.

"Nervous," I said.

Thank God. Only one fell out.

He rubbed the hood onto the sides of his face, concealing most of his features. It was unzipped, and he wore a ribbed tank top underneath. From what I could see, he was built like an athlete. I sat and stared as I admired his eyes, body and smile. I tried my best not to speak.

"Sorry, I didn't mean to startle you or make you nervous. Do you remember me?"

My head bobbed up and down like one of those little dogs in the back window of some old person's car. Nervously, I rubbed the wrinkles from my skirt. Perspiration formed on my palms like cold can of beer on a hot Austin day.

Kace, you look like an idiot, say something.

"Eyes, grey. Grey. I like your eyes. Your eyes," I took a breath, raised my eyebrows and pointed at my mouth as I pursed my lips.

I took another deep breath and exhaled slowly.

"I'm nervous too, if it helps," he said as he smiled sweetly and leaned onto the upper portion of my reception station.

I raised my eyebrows and kept my mouth closed.

"I am. You can kind of tell when I'm nervous or I don't want to talk about something. I pull the hood over my head. My name is Shane. Shane Dekkar," he said as he pulled the hood from his face.

Holy book fucking boyfriend. This guy is perfect.

I grabbed a sticky note and scribbled on it with my pen.

When I get nervous or really excited the words don't come out in order.
It's embarrassing.
I'm sorry.

I handed him the note.

He looked down, read it, and smiled as he looked up from the note. He turned the note over face down, reached down onto my lower desk, and grabbed a pen from my jar of pens. He scribbled on the back side of the note and handed it to me.

WHEN I GET NERVOUS I HIDE
UNDER MY HOOD.

WHAT'S YOUR NAME?

I set the note aside and grabbed a new one. I wrote on it and handed it back to him.

> My name is spelled Kace.
> It's pronounced Casey, but
> spelled weird. My friends
> call me Kace without the
> "Y" pronounced. I go by
> either. I like your eyes.

He read the note, turned it over, and chuckled. He looked up at the ceiling as if he were thinking, and wrote on the back side of the note. As he handed it to me, he stared into my eyes. I reached for the note and smiled as he released it to me.

> I HAVE SO MUCH TO SAY I WOULD LIKE ONE OF THE BIG SHEETS FROM YOUR LEGAL PAD ON YOUR LEFT. FOR NOW, I WILL SAY THIS.
>
> I LIKE YOUR FACE. YOU'RE BEAUTIFUL. AND, IF YOU EVER GET CONFUSED AND CAN'T TALK, TAP YOUR HAND ONCE FOR YES, AND TWICE FOR NO.

This was so exciting.

I ripped a sheet from the legal pad and handed it to him. The anticipation of what he might write on the sheet was killing me. Hopefully he would write a lot of things on the sheet. I pushed the two yellow sticky notes aside and set my water bottle upright. I looked up at him as he thought and wrote slowly. He folded the sheet in half and handed it to me.

I unfolded it and was pleased to see that he had filled almost the entire page with hand written questions. His penmanship was perfect.

KACE,

I'M SHANE DEKKAR. WE SAW EACH OTHER THE FIRST
TIME AT THE DRUG STORE PARKING LOT. I WALKED
BY HERE A MONTH OR SO AGO AND NOTICED YOU
FOR A SECOND TIME. YOUR HAIR WAS REALLY SHINY. I
THINK EVERYTHING HAPPENS FOR A REASON. I FEEL
I REALLY NEED TO FIND OUT WHO YOU ARE. I FOUND
IT INCREASINGLY DIFFICULT TO KNOW YOU WERE HERE
AND NOT COME SEE YOU, SO I CAME IN TODAY TO
SEE MY INSURANCE AGENT AND SAY HELLO TO YOU. I
HAVE SOME QUESTIONS. HERE THEY ARE.

WAS THAT GUY AT THE DRUGSTORE YOUR BOYFRIEND?

IS HE VIOLENT TOWARD YOU, OR WERE YOU REALLY
JUST IN A LITTLE ARGUMENT?

ARE YOU SINGLE?

AVAILABLE?

DO YOU LIKE TURKEY SANDWICHES?

HAVE YOU EATEN LUNCH?

WOULD YOU LIKE TO GO TO LUNCH?

ARE YOU A RUNNER?

I read what he wrote and read it again. *Your hair was really shiny.* Could this guy be any cuter than this?

I looked up at him and started to write a response beside the questions he had written. I thought carefully as I wrote.

WAS THAT GUY AT THE DRUGSTORE YOUR BOYFRIEND?
Yes, but I want to find a way out.

I read the next question and struggled with what I should write. I considered writing several things, but opted for a one word answer.

IS HE VIOLENT TOWARD YOU, OR WERE YOU REALLY JUST IN A LITTLE ARGUMENT? Argument.

ARE YOU SINGLE? See above.

AVAILABLE? I think maybe.

DO YOU LIKE TURKEY SANDWICHES? Haha. Love them.

HAVE YOU EATEN LUNCH? No.

WOULD YOU LIKE TO GO TO LUNCH? I think yes.

ARE YOU A RUNNER? Yes, I am.

I looked at my watch. It was 10:45 already. I scribbled my own note onto the bottom of the sheet.

This was fun.

I get off for lunch at 11:30 and can be gone for an hour. The diner across the street has good turkey sandwiches. You can meet me there. Do you always wear a hoodie? It's hot outside. I'm not as nervous now, but still kind of.

You make my palms sweaty.

I read what I wrote, smiled, and handed it back to him.

He read the note, folded it and stuck it in his back pocket. He reached back and pulled the hood over his head and smiled. As he placed his forearms onto the upper countertop, he leaned forward slowly, getting closer to my face.

His eyes commanded my attention.

"I'll see you at eleven thirty. I'm glad I make your hands sweaty. I always wear a hoodie. Well, almost always. You don't need to respond if you're still nervous," he whispered.

Almost unknowingly, I found myself leaning closer to him as he spoke. His breath smelled sweet.

"Turkey," I blurted.

Are you fucking kidding me? Turkey? That's all you can come up with?

I rolled my eyes and pointed to my mouth.

"Turkey," his sweet breath whispered.

47

He leaned a little closer. I leaned toward him a little more.

"Get your little sticky note pad and get a new note, Kace. Write this on it. I'm coming, Kace. *I'm coming for your heart.*"

As he turned and walked away, I stood up and faced him.

And I melted a little.

Good lord.

Wow.

I could just watch him walk forever.

Kace,

I'm coming for
your heart.

SHANE

I've spent most of my adult life *wanting* to be in a meaningful relationship. The relationships we typically have in high school never really amount to anything meaningful, and I didn't look at my high school relationships as being anything but relationship curiosity. To think as a high school student we have any idea of what we want, need, or really desire in a life-long mate is ridiculous at best.

I had a relationship as an adult for several years with Tina. She and I were inseparable. She spent all of her spare time with me, and I did the same with her. She spent considerable time at the gym watching me train. I suspected we would get married and spend our lives together. Being around her made me feel as if my life were in order.

One day, she came home and told me - with much excitement - she had been accepted into the Navy. I was beyond shocked. After a lengthy discussion, I found out she had been trying to pass the entrance examinations for a few years. She never bothered to tell me her desire to join the military - and after the relationship ended, it seemed cheap and worthless.

Since the relationship ended, I had no intent to actively pursue a female companion of any kind. I figured I'd spend the rest of my life focused on boxing and being single. I expressed no desire to be in any

49

form of a relationship since Tina, and I had serious doubts this would ever change.

Meeting Kace was refreshing and strange at the same time. I had never met a woman who immediately possessed my thoughts the way she did. Even after meeting for the first time in the parking lot, I found myself thinking about her often. I wondered if she was happy, safe, and most of all - single. Seeing her for the second time when I went to pay my insurance made me wonder about our meeting being fate.

My grandfather always told me God puts people in our lives for a reason. It's our responsibility to recognize them for what he intends them to be to us. Some people are bad, and we need to recognize them as such. The bad people or events in life allow us to have an accurate means of measuring the good. Other people are good, and may have something to offer us. They may make our lives, minds or basic understanding richer. Now, by a basis of comparison, we are able to see the difference between good and evil. If something or someone is presented to us once, we will often dismiss it as being nothing more than happenstance. If that person or situation is presented twice, it is God slapping us in the face and telling us to *pay attention.* It is fate.

I believe in fate.

Looking through the window toward the office building, I took a drink of my water. As she began to cross the street, I felt my heart race. I stood up and watched her cross the street. Smiling, she waited for a break in traffic. She was wearing a black pencil skirt, heels, and a tangerine colored sleeveless top. Clearly and without any effort whatsoever, she defined beauty as she gracefully ran across the street in her high heels.

As she hopped over the curb and onto the sidewalk, she rubbed her hands on her skirt. Her hair appeared to be naturally blonde, and bounced as she walked down the sidewalk toward the door. As the bell which hung over the entrance chimed, I sat back into my seat.

I leaned forward in the booth and turned her direction. As she made eye contact, I waved. She smiled and slowly walked my direction. She was simply adorable.

As she approached the booth, I stood from my seat and inched between the table and seat toward the aisle. I stood in the aisle, looked down at my raggedy boots, and glanced up at her. Standing about a foot in front of me, she rubbed her hands on her skirt and stared into my eyes, smiling. Slowly, she raised her right hand between us, and waved. Not certain if she could speak intelligibly or not, I pointed to the other side of the booth.

She stepped away from me and walked to the other side of the booth.

"I got you a bottle of water, sit down. Relax," I said softly.

She placed her purse in the seat and slid into the booth beside it. She twisted the lid off of the bottle of water and took a long drink, raising her eyebrows and focusing on me as she did. As she placed the bottle and the lid onto the table, she took a deep breath.

"Hopefully," she smiled and flipped her hair over her shoulder

"My mouth and brain will stay," she paused.

"Connected," she smiled as she exhaled.

I pulled my hands from my hoodie pockets and lightly clapped. She rested her elbows on the table and patted her hands together in a mimicking fashion until I stopped. When I stopped clapping she placed her hands in her lap and smiled.

I pressed my forearms onto the edge of the table and leaned her direction, "You're adorable."

Without speaking, her mouth formed the words, *thank you.*

"Just in case you get mixed up with your words - one tap always means yes, two means no, remember?" I said.

"Okay," she laughed.

"Would you two like to order?" the waitress asked.

I held my index finger in the air and focused on Kace, "Give us a few minutes, please."

"I'll check back in a couple," the waitress smiled.

"Okay, I'll start at the beginning," I took a deep breath, exhaled, and shoved my hands deep into my pockets of the hoodie.

"I'm going to guess, based on the fact that there was an empty yogurt container in the trash at your desk, and there was a plastic spoon in the container, you normally eat at your office. You probably save all of the money you're supposed to eat out with and use it for yourself. I'm also going to guess what I thought was an iPad that your douchebag boyfriend smashed in the parking lot was a Kindle. And the Kindle in your purse was one you bought to replace the one that he smashed," I took another breath.

"And you probably read as much as you can - to dream. To dream of what *could* be. You live through the characters in the books you read, and it allows you to have some form of solace, or an inner peace in your otherwise worthless existence of a life with the douchebag," I paused and looked at Kace.

Her eyes wide and her mouth slightly open, she stared at me, speechless.

"He's controlling, isn't he?'

She nodded her head like it was on a spring.

I shook my head from side to side and pulled my hood over my shoulders. As I pressed my hood against my face, I clenched my jaw.

"Are you…" she looked up at the ceiling and tilted her head to the side.

"Mad…" she paused and took a short shallow breath.

"At me?" she said softly.

This woman was the definition of beauty. Clearly. She also possessed every quality which made her as adorable in regard to personality anyone could ever wish for. Even through her little speech problem, she maintained a smile and a positive attitude. I wanted to crush the asshole that was abusing her.

I shook my head slowly and accidentally growled.

Just a little.

"No, not at all. I'm sorry. It makes me angry when I find out someone is abusing a woman. Well, women, kids and old people - people who are incapable of providing much resistance. I couldn't even tell you how many women I have talked to who are just like you. The eating at work, saving money, hiding things for fear of getting in trouble," I paused and rolled my eyes.

"You'd be surprised at how many women are in relationships just like yours. It makes me sick," I clenched my jaw in anger.

A slight frown washed over her face. Obviously she had become embarrassed.

"Let's talk about something else," I said as I pulled my hands from my hoodie pockets.

She shook her head from side-to-side.

Loudly, she tapped the table twice.

"You want to talk about this?" I asked.

She tapped the table once.

"How long have you been with him?'

"Sixteen," she responded.

I shook my head, "Ever been with anyone else?"

She shook her head slowly and took a drink of her water.

"You guys ready?" the waitress asked.

I looked at the waitress and turned toward Kace. She nodded and smiled.

"Turkey sandwich on," I paused and looked at Kace.

"Wheat," she said.

"Two turkey sandwiches on wheat bread – add a salad to each. With vinaigrette on the side please. Thank you," I smiled.

"Dressing on the sandwich?" The waitress asked.

I looked at Kace.

"Light mayonnaise, please," she said softly.

"Same," I said.

"Okay, just a few minutes," the waitress said.

"You feeling less nervous?" I asked.

"It's weird. Yes, I am. When you ordered the dressing on the side, I think I realized you're human. I don't know, I just immediately felt comfortable. It was like my insides sighed. Would you have ordered light mayonnaise if I hadn't said something?" she asked.

Wow, she speaks.

"Yes, I would have," I responded.

She sighed softly and smiled.

"You're beautiful, Kace. When you're lying in bed tonight, remember that. You're beautiful," I looked into her eyes and said.

She smiled.

"You are?" I asked as I motioned toward her with my right hand.

She shrugged.

"Beautiful," I said again.

"You are?" I asked.

She slowly smiled.

"Beautiful?" she asked softly.

"Let's try this again," I said.

"Kace, what are you? Describe yourself to me?"

"Beautiful," she responded softly as she smiled.

"You certainly are. Don't forget it, okay?" I said, nodding my head once sharply.

She nodded and took a deep breath.

"So, he's controlling. He's abusive. He slaps me. He hits me. He yells at me, chokes me, he tells me I can't leave the house. Let's see," she paused, looked out the window and bobbed her head up and down along with the music playing.

"He monitors my text messages, phone calls, spending, and tells me I'm a dirty slut and a whore," she turned and looked back in my direction.

Her eyes were welled with tears, but none fell.

I gritted my teeth and tried not to show my anger. People like Kace's husband made me develop an anger only fed by action or resolving the situation. When I box, I often tell myself my opponent is abusing a woman. It allows me to become at peace with fighting someone who hasn't really done anything to deserve the beating they are about to receive.

"Have you cheated on him?" I asked.

"Oh heck no," she said.

"You're not married?" I asked.

"No, thank God," she shook her head and wiped her eyes.

"Do you believe in fate?" I asked.

"I suppose so," she paused.

"What do you mean?" she asked.

"Well, I moved here two years ago from Compton, California. I bumped into you at the drug store. Then I saw you again at the office across the street. I couldn't get you off of my mind. It's as if you were pumping through my veins, like you had infected me. Meeting you once might have been an accident, maybe happenstance. But meeting you twice, it's fate. I don't know where this will end up, but I'll spend the rest of my life trying to find out," I reached into my hood and rubbed my hair with my hands.

"Yeah, Austin is a huge city. I suppose running into me twice would be almost impossible. So, you came here from Compton? Isn't that like the ghetto?" she asked.

"My father was an active duty Marine, so I lived with my grandfather. He had lived there for decades and refused to move. But yeah, it's the ghetto. It kind of made me who I am, I suppose," I pushed the hood off of my head and rubbed my hair with my fingertips.

"Here's your lunch," the waitress said as she sat the plates down.

"Thank you, ma'am," I said as she stepped back from the booth.

The waitress looked at me and smiled. She was tall, thin, and probably in her mid-fifties. Her skin was very tan, probably from the countless hours she spent after work relaxing in the sun. More than likely she was single and r4ecovering from a relationship similar to Kace's. Most of the older waitresses in diners seemed to be. As I returned the smile she turned and walked away.

"So is your father out of the military now?" Kace asked.

"No, he was killed in Afghanistan doing what he loved; fighting," I said.

"I'm so sorry," she said, her hands cupped over her mouth.

I looked out the window.

"Don't be. He begged to go back, each time. He knew nothing else. He couldn't make sense of being here in the United States after his first tour. I think it was the only way he could make the war seem like it was right or *just*. Anyway, he died doing what he loved," I turned from the window and focused on her face.

"So, can you leave him and go live with your parents?" I asked.

"No. He hasn't let me see either of my parents for years. My relationship with them has deteriorated. He hates both of my parents. I think they hate him," she said as she picked up her sandwich.

She was so matter of fact about everything - like it really didn't matter. This piece of shit of a human being had manipulated and controlled her to a point that she really didn't realize everything he had done to her.

"He doesn't *let* you see your parents?" I asked, shocked at this statement.

"No," she responded, shaking her head.

"He doesn't *let* you. *Interesting*. What's his name?" I asked.

"Josh," she responded after finishing her bite of sandwich.

I shook my head and unzipped my hoodie. The more I thought about this guy, the hotter it seemed to get.

"What are you, Kace?" I asked.

She looked at me with a confused look on her face, and then appeared she had a revelation.

"Beautiful," she grinned.

"Yes you are. Don't forget it, okay?" I asked.

She nodded and blushed slightly.

"Now back to Josh. I'm going to call him *Buster*. I had a friend in Compton named Josh. He was a pretty good guy. From here on out, I'm going to call him Buster," I said as I reached for my sandwich.

"Buster," she laughed.

She studied me and smiled, "I like that. Well, you know what I mean. Yeah, *Buster*. It fits."

"So are you a personal trainer or something?" she asked.

"No, I'm a boxer," I responded as I handed her a napkin.

She smiled and slid the napkin beside her plate. Her teeth were snow white and perfectly shaped.

With my index finger, I pointed to the corner of my mouth and then to her face. She raised the napkin and wiped her mouth.

"Light on the mayonnaise," I chuckled.

"Excuse me, did you say boxer? Like, you *box*? What do you do for work?" she asked, her face filled with wonder.

"I box. I'm a fighter, it's what I do," I responded.

"Oh God," she responded.

Quickly, she stood from her seat and stared at me.

"What?" I asked as I stood up.

"Bathroom. Bye," she stammered.

Hurriedly, she pushed herself out of the booth, and ran toward the bathroom.

Feeling somewhat confused, I pulled the hood over my head and sat back down. I started thinking of Kace, her boyfriend, and a way to get them apart. Ultimately, it needed to happen. Whether Kace ended up with me, alone or with someone else did not matter. Getting her out of the abusive relationship she was in did.

"Is your girlfriend okay?" the waitress asked.

"She's not my girlfriend, but I think so, why?" I asked.

"Oh, she just ran to the bathroom like something was wrong," she answered.

"Well, I think she just had to go really bad," I chuckled.

"Need anything else?" she asked as she pulled the bill from her apron.

"No, how much is it?" I asked.

"$21.30 with the salads," she responded, looking at the receipt.

I leaned forward and removed my wallet from my pocket. I flipped through the bills, and removed a fifty dollar bill.

"Here you go, keep the change," I said.

"Uhhm, this is a fifty," she said, showing me the bill.

"I know. Keep the change. And thank you," I said as I nodded my head and sat back down into the seat.

"Oh God. Wow. Thank you," she said, smiling.

Her teeth glistened.

"Certainly," I nodded and pulled my hood off of my head as I spoke.

As she turned to walk away, Kace slid back into her seat.

"You alright?" I asked, laughing lightly and shaking my head.

She nodded excitedly.

"What happened?" I asked.

She pointed at me.

"What?" I asked.

She clenched her fists and acted as if she was throwing punches slowly at the center of the table.

"Boxing? Me?" I asked.

She nodded.

I remembered what she said about getting nervous, and the fact it embarrassed her to speak. I felt bad about making her nervous. Some people simply aren't cut out for the violence associated with the sport.

"I'm sorry if I made you nervous, I didn't mean to. It's all I know. It's my profession, not a hobby," I said apologetically.

She shook her head and once again began to throw fake punches slowly at the center of the table.

Somewhat confused, I looked at her and thought about what she had written down earlier.

When I get nervous or really excited the words don't come out in order. It's embarrassing. I'm sorry.

"Excited?" I asked.

She nodded her head repeatedly and shook her fists.

Here's my opportunity to seal the deal.

"Well, I can't wait to beat Buster's ass, make you mine, and take you to a fight. You'll love it, I'm undefeated. Never been beat," I bragged as I pulled my hoodie over my shoulders.

I stood in the booth and tossed my hoodie in the seat beside me. Now standing in my ribbed tank top, I flexed my pectoral muscles and slowly sat down.

"It's hot in here. Do you think it's hot in here?" I asked, scrunching my eyebrows.

Her mouth open wide, she nodded her head sharply as she stood. She inched her way out of the booth, and turned to face me. In somewhat of a daze, she stared at my chest and biceps for a split second, and took off in a dead run for the bathroom.

I turned and looked out the window at the office where Kace worked and chuckled to myself.

I suspect she was considering what was in her best interest. Most women in her position merely needed a little shoulder to lean on through the course of change. After the fact, they almost immediately realized it was something they should have done long before. For them, making the initial move was difficult to do without assistance and encouragement. I intended to provide both.

Now I needed to figure a way to get rid of Buster and convince Kace it was what was best for her.

I felt as if someone was behind me, and I turned to face the aisle. As I did, Kace picked up my hoodie and tossed it over the table to her seat. She slid along the seat of the booth until she was against my arm. She turned and looked up at me and smiled, resting her head on my bicep.

As she leaned against me, I noticed she was about a foot shorter than I was.

I love short women.

And the thought of beating Buster's ass.

KACE

Talking to Shane made me feel like a woman again. He was nice to me because he was a nice person. He thought I was pretty. He told me I was beautiful. Since we met at the diner, we had been communicating through my gmail account on my phone, because *Buster* couldn't trace it.

I really liked calling Josh *Buster* in my head. I was afraid I would accidentally do it one time to his face. Shane told me to find a way to leave Josh even if it didn't include thoughts of Shane and I being together. He said I needed to find a way to leave him for myself, and not for the reward of being with someone else or the thought of having a relationship with him.

He explained I needed to do it for *me*. It seemed easy, and as much as I had grown to hate Josh, it was almost incomprehensible for me to think of leaving him. When I thought of it my head spun in circles. I could think of one reason to leave him and about a hundred reasons to stay.

Change scared me. It scared me to death. What if this. What if that. Even though Josh was a prick and he treated me like shit, I have a home with him. And I can always come home. Home, for me, is a comfortable place. If someone could just decide for me it would make everything so much easier. For me to decide might take forever, maybe even a little bit longer than forever.

On the weekends, Josh often left for a good part of the day. He rarely took me with him. When I would ask him where he was going, his answer was generally *out*.

When he left, I usually baked.

Baking made me happy. I enjoyed baking things. It satisfied me greatly to have someone eat what I prepared and tell me they liked it. When I got upset I baked far more than normal. The baking settled me down and allowed me to feel as if I was accomplishing something. Maybe it was because there was a beginning and an end to it. Maybe I enjoyed creating it from my own mind. My hands creating something allowed me to feel a degree of accomplishment.

Maybe it was all of those things combined.

I was baking pecan and butterscotch chip cookies for Josh. They were his favorite. I had no idea why I was still concerned with making something Josh liked. I never eat this shit. I baked it and he ate it. He took cookies in his lunch, ate them in bed, and ate on the couch while he played video games.

Josh was disgusting.

I pulled the cookies from the oven and set them on the rack to cool. The Tupperware I was placing the cookies in was almost full. Six dozen cookies was a lot of cookies, but not for Josh. He would eat six dozen cookies in about three days or so.

Josh is fat and disgusting.

Shane isn't.

Every morning, Shane called me at work and we would talk for a few minutes. I couldn't talk on my cell phone, so he would call me on my work phone. We talked about everything and about nothing. Sometimes I would just sit and listen to him talk or listen to him breathe. Knowing he was there was enough. Someone who wouldn't treat me like shit. Someone who actually cared.

My time with Shane was valuable to me. If I didn't get to talk to him it was disappointing. It wasn't that I was disappointed in him - it was just let down if it didn't happen. It had become so easy to enjoy his time, and I could do it without worry or effort. Shane didn't judge me. And he never said anything bad to me.

I removed the cookies from the sheet with the spatula and placed them in the Tupperware. There was almost no dough left and the container was full, so I began washing out the bowl. As I was cleaning the bowl in the sink, I heard the key in the door. My muscles tensed and I started shaking.

Buster.

"What the fuck, did this sum bitch catch fire while I was gone?" he bellowed from the doorway.

"I cooked your favorite cookies," I said as he walked into the kitchen.

"No bake?" he asked.

You hate no bake cookies, you miserable asshole.

"No, the butterscotch with pecans," I turned from the sink and smiled.

He reached into the Tupperware container and took a handful of cookies. As he walked to the refrigerator, I could smell the beer on his breath. *Perfect, he's drunk.* I started shaking even worse as I rinsed the bowl in the sink. As he reached into the refrigerator, I began to dry the bowl.

"You drink my fuckin' beer, you whore?" he asked, his head stuffed in the refrigerator.

"I don't drink beer, Josh. You know that," I responded.

"Don't back talk me you slut," he said as he shut the refrigerator door.

"Somebody drank 'em. There's only five left. I had a twelver in that 'fridge," he said as he opened the can of beer.

"Only you and I are in the house, Josh. So if they're gone, you drank them," I said softly as I dried the bowl with the dish towel.

"You callin' me stupid?" he asked.

"No," I looked down at the floor.

"Well, I know who lives here. And I know what I drunk and I know what I didn't. Who you had in here while I was gone?" he asked as he stuffed another cookie in his mouth.

"No one, Josh," I answered.

"Now you wanna lie," he said as he tipped his beer can up to his mouth.

"Back talk me and lie. Somebody has been up in this bitch. My fuckin' beer is *gone*. Now tell me who," he demanded.

"No one," I repeated. He was scaring me. I really didn't want to be hit.

"Then where's my beer?" he screamed.

Sometimes we make decisions and we think the decisions we make are to our benefit. Other times, we make decisions and at the time we make them, they seem to be what makes sense, and later we find out they weren't such a good idea. Being able to discern the good decisions from the bad decisions, in advance, would be priceless.

"I drank them," I said.

"How you gonna pay to replace them, you dumb whore? I knew

you were drinkin' my beers. Probably drank that fuckin' Jack too, didn't ya?"

I nodded.

I didn't see it coming, but I felt the impact. His hand hit my face so hard everything went black. I spun in a circle and landed on the floor. When I could see again, I was on the floor and he was hovering over me with his fists clenched.

"You can drink my beers and you'll pay me for 'em. But no one fucks with my Jack. You know that. I knew you drunk it you little drunken whore," he screamed as he grabbed a handful of my hair and pulled me to my feet.

"Josh, no! I didn't drink them," I cried, my hair pulled tight by his left hand.

"Well, either way, you're lying. You said you did, you said you didn't. One's a lie," he stuffed a cookie in his mouth and took a drink of beer.

Smack!

He hit me harder than he had ever hit me before. I didn't know what he hit me with, but my mouth hurt like hell. I could taste blood. I pushed the back of my teeth with my tongue. One was loose.

I opened my eyes. Everything was blurry. My lips already felt ten times bigger than normal. As I cried and sobbed, he pulled me toward the refrigerator by my hair. Grabbing the back of my hair in his hand, he opened the refrigerator door and shoved my head inside.

"How many beers you see up in this motherfucker?" he screamed.

I blinked and looked inside. I could see nothing. My eyes wouldn't focus.

He said he had five earlier...

"Four," I guessed.

"See any Jack?" he screamed.

"No," I answered.

He pulled me down to the floor by my hair and shoved me with his hand, sending me across the floor on my back. I relaxed on the floor, lying on my back crying. I turned my head to the side so I could still see him. The pain in my face and mouth was unbearable.

I watched his hand as he reached into the refrigerator. I heard him open another beer and take a very long series of drinks.

"Know why?" he asked.

"Why what?" I asked.

"What the fuck we talking about, you dumb cunt?" he screamed.

"Josh, I don't know. I'm scared. You hit me, I'm hurt and bleeding. Please…"

"I don't give a fuck if you're bleedin'. The Jack! The fucking Jack Daniels, Kace. You know why you don't see it?" he screamed.

"No?" I answered, confused.

"Cause you drunk it," he screamed.

I saw the blur of his boot and thought he was stepping over me to go to the other room.

KACE

When I woke up, my face felt as if it were stuck to the tile floor. I lifted my head from the large spot of dried blood on. My mouth was throbbing. I reached toward my face and felt my lips. They were both mangled. I had a piece of Josh's boot heel in my mouth. I spit it onto the floor.

White.

I picked it up and looked at it. I blinked and looked again.

Oh no.

He didn't.

I circled my tongue around my front teeth. It caught on an opening in the front.

I looked at what I held in my hand.

That motherfucker kicked my tooth out.

I could hear the video game playing as he screamed in the other room. I looked around the kitchen. Two empty beer cans sat on the kitchen counter. The cookies were gone. My bowl sat on top of the counter where I had left it.

Who beats their girlfriend to a pulp on the floor, kicks her teeth out, and then takes a beer and cookies into the other room to play video games while she lie in a puddle of blood on the floor?

Fucking Buster. That's who.

I stuck my tooth in my jeans pocket.

I picked up the bowl and felt it in my hands.

Not heavy enough.

I opened the bottom cabinet and looked inside. I quietly pulled the largest cast-iron skillet from the cabinet. *Oh yeah. This should work.* I tip-toed out of the kitchen and to the rear of the living room. He was sitting on the couch, facing the television and playing video games. His back was toward me.

This could be just perfect.

Fucking cocksucker.

I could see the back of his head over the top of the couch. I knew if I *walked* in behind him, he might see me and catch me. As he screamed at the television, I ran as fast as I could toward him - the cast-iron skillet held high above my head with both hands. As he looked to his right, his mouth began to open and his eyes were as big as saucers.

The skillet came down hard. When it hit his forehead, it made an awful thud. I hated to, but I smiled when it bounced off of his head.

I stood over him and admired my handy work.

I dropped the skillet on the floor behind the couch and looked at him. His forehead already developed a knot the size of half a baseball. His head was split open, but not as bad as my lips were. I looked at him and how he was slumped into the couch and shook my head. Although my heart was beating at a very rapid pace, I was surprisingly calm.

I walked to my bedroom and grabbed my purse, Kindle, and cell phone. I walked into the living room and checked Josh. He was still unconscious. I reached down on the floor and grabbed the cast iron skillet and took it with me as I walked into the bedroom again.

I opened the closet door and pulled out the largest piece of luggage

I had. I unzipped it and began stuffing all of my work clothes into it. I ran to the dresser and grabbed socks, panties, and shirts. When the bag was almost full, I shoved in as many pairs of shoes as I could. I zipped the luggage and drug it into the other room.

Still unconscious.

I dropped the luggage on the floor and walked back into the bedroom and grabbed the skillet.

Slowly, I walked toward the couch. I reached down and picked up his cell phone from the floor. I stepped back and thought as I looked at him sprawled out on the couch. The crotch of his pants was soaked.

Fuck this asshole.

I leaned over his body and pushed my hand into his pants pocket. *There we go.* I pulled out the keys to his truck. I looked to the side of the couch toward where he had removed his boots and smiled. I slid my purse over my shoulder and walked toward his boots. I dropped the keys and phone into his boots and picked them up. I walked back, grabbed the luggage, and pulled it behind me to the front door. As I opened the front door, I looked around the house. I needed nothing else. I guess, ultimately, what Shane had said was right.

When walking away from something we were once committed to, we often hesitate. Deciding to make a major change in life is difficult. But we all reach a point when we're done. Done giving to a world that only takes. Until then, you'll want, you'll wait, and you'll contemplate change. When you're truly done, you'll know. You'll know when the time comes.

You'll know when the time comes.

The time has come.

SHANE

"Hand me those tongs, this side of the chicken is done," I said toward Ripp.

"Fuck, I don't know where they are," he screamed back.

"They're right beside you, Jesus," I hollered as I held the lid of the barbeque grill in the air, "right where you set them. And why the fuck are we screaming?"

He turned and looked at the table on the edge of the deck. As he reached for the tongs, my phone rang.

"Phone's ringing, Dekk," he screamed as he tossed me the tongs.

I grasped each piece of chicken with the tongs, and flipped them over on the grill. Ripp and I had somewhat of a tradition of eating barbequed chicken every Saturday evening. I loved to eat healthy, and enjoyed our tradition. Ripp wasn't as concerned as I was with food, and typically would eat whatever someone handed him. He worked harder in his exercise routines to get rid of it.

I used this as a means of making him eat healthy. It was my way of letting him relax a little from his rigorous exercise regimen.

I closed the lid of the grill and pulled my phone from my pocket. *Kace.*

Okay, this is weird. She never calls or texts.

I pushed redial and called her phone back.

"Who was it?" Ripp asked.

"Kace," I said and turned to face away from him.

She answered the phone and began to talk a hundred miles an hour. I could understand about every other word.

"Slow down…slow down, what's wrong?" I asked.

"I left," she responded.

"Like left, left?" I asked.

"Left, left," she responded.

"Can I come to where you are? Juth for a little bit? I need to thee you," she asked.

"Are you okay?" I asked as I turned to face Ripp.

I placed my hand over the mouth piece of the phone.

"Can she come here for a bit?" I whispered toward Ripp

He shrugged his shoulders, turned his palms up, and nodded his head.

"Yeah you can come here, you have a way to write down the address?" I asked.

"Tetht it to me," she said.

"Your voice sounds funny, you have a lisp," I said.

"I'll tell you about it when I get there," she said.

"Alright, I'll text it to you. Who's the most beautiful woman in the world," I asked.

"Right now, I hath no idea. I'll thee you in a minute," she laughed.

She hung up and I placed my phone in my pocket. We had never seen each other on the weekends, only during lunch at the diner across the street from her office. My mind raced. I thought of all of the possibilities. It had been about a month since we first met at the diner, and I knew she was becoming fond of me – she never hesitated to tell me.

I suspected there had to be something to drive her over the edge. Her lisp had me worried. I stood and stared at the barbeque grill.

"Dekk, you alright?" Ripp asked as he walked up to my side.

"Yeah. Yeah, I think so," I responded.

"You sure? Your friend alright?" he asked as he opened the grill.

"I don't know. I have a feeling something happened," I responded.

"Like?" he asked.

"I don't know. But I know this. If she so much as has a fingerprint on her, I'm going to go beat the brakes off of that dirt bag. Where's my fucking hoodie?" I asked.

"It's on the lounge," Ripp responded as he pointed toward the lounge chair.

"Brother, if he touched a hair on her head, you'll have to beat me to him. I'll beat his ass for you. Until he's a pile of bones. No one beats a woman that I know about. Not and gets away with it. So, I got this, Dekk. *I got it.* Just because that's how we do it here in Texas," he laughed.

"I'm serious," I said.

"So am I," he responded as extended his arm and made a clenched fist.

He nodded toward his hand.

"C'mon do it," he said.

I gritted my teeth and made a fist.

He nodded his head again, "I got this."

I bumped his fist with mine.

And I knew.

Ripp had my back.

KACE

We make decisions which may impact or have an effect on our lives, and at times we regret or past decisions. I try to live my life without regret. There have been plenty of times I wish my life were different, but I refuse to regret the path I have traveled to get me where I am today.

I looked into the the rearview mirror. My face was covered in blood. My lips split open, my tooth was missing and my hair was lightly matted with blood.

I smiled. Immediately, I winced from the pain of my split lips.

I pulled my car in the driveway, checked the address, backed up and parked in the street in front of the house. I looked at the text message again.

724 All Hallows. We're in the back on the deck. Gate is unlocked.

I sat in my car looking like a murder victim who had survived and was happier than I had ever been in my life. My only regret was I didn't hit Josh in the head with the skillet ten years prior. I opened the car door and took a deep breath. *Just as well get this over with.* I stepped out and started walking up the driveway toward the gate in the fence. I reached for the handle, took another deep breath, exhaled, and pulled the gate open.

I stood at the opened gate and stared.

"Hey babe. So what's going on?" Shane asked from the top of the deck as he started walking in my direction. As he got closer to me, his eyes opened wide. His face filled with surprise. His lips began to quiver. He stood in front of me and slowly reached out to move my hair from my cheeks. He lowered his face toward mine and looked into my eyes.

"What the *fuck* happened to you? Car wreck?" he said in a calm but stern tone.

I stood and stared at the deck, incapable of speaking.

Holy Mary mother of Christ himself.

"Ripp, get over here, I think she's in shock. She's been in a wreck or something," he said over his shoulder.

"Holy fuck. I'll call an ambulance," the shirtless man said.

I shook my head.

"No," I blurted, "It duthen't hurt anymore. Juth lookth bad. Leth wipe it off, maybe."

"Babe, you're in shock. We'll get an ambulance," he said softly as he pushed my hair over my ears.

"Ambulanthe," I muttered.

"No!" I screamed.

Shane jumped back.

"Ith not bad, juth lookth bad," I shook my head.

"Not a wreck. Buth-ter," I sighed.

Frantically, I waved my hands in front of me and pointed to my mouth.

"Babe, I can see. Your lips. And I see the tooth babe. We'll get thiat prick, don't worry. We got this. It will *never* happen again," he assured me.

As he looked at my face and moved my hair to the side, I heard a rumbling tone coming from his chest.

He was growling.

"Where's my fucking phone, Dekk?" the shirtless man screamed.

Please don't come over here.

"Fuck, I'm brain dead. Mine's in my pocket. Here," Shane said as he pulled his phone from his pocket and held it beside his waist. His hands were shaking.

I reached out and slapped the phone from his hand, knocking it to the ground.

"Babe, we need to call an ambulance, you're in shock," he said as he bent down to pick up the phone.

I kicked it across the concrete patio before he touched it.

"Thirt. Tattooth," I whimpered helplessly as I pointed to the shirtless man.

He scrunched his brow and looked confused. He turned and looked at the shirtless man, who was walking in our direction.

"Dude, I can't find it. Where's yours?" he asked as he put his hand on Shane's shoulder.

I crossed my legs and waved my arms.

Shane's mouth slowly formed a smile. He shook his head.

"Ripp, go put on a shirt," Shane said as he smiled at me.

I nodded over and over, *and then I remembered.*

I reached over and tapped his shoulder once.

"Dude, it's a hundred and five degrees. I ain't putting on a shirt," he said.

Shane took off his hoodie and handed it over his shoulder to the other man. He maintained eye contact with me the entire time, smiling.

He's proud of me for remembering to tap him once.

"Don't ask, Ripp. For *me*, put it on, *please*," Shane said softly.

"Alright, Dekk. Damn, my bad," he said as he pulled the hoodie over his shoulders.

He stood with the hoodie unzipped. It barely covered half of him. His chest and stomach were exposed. His stomach muscles rippled. Hints of tattoos on his chest were exposed.

I pointed to the other man and shook my head. I motioned with my hands as if I were zipping the hoodie. Shane slowly turned and looked at the other man.

"Zip it up, Ripp. *Damn*," he said.

"It's too fucking small," he complained.

"It's an extra fucking large. You're just too god damned big. She's fucking bleeding and can't speak. Zip the damned thing up. Son of a bitch, Ripp. I told you she has anxiety. She can't talk because you're fucking distracting the shit out of her," he started laughing as he spoke.

He zipped the hoodie up to his neck, turned and walked to the upper wooden deck.

I exhaled.

I closed my eyes and nodded my head slowly. I took a slow breath and exhaled. I opened my eyes and pointed to the deck. Shane turned and put his right arm over my shoulder and his left behind my legs. Swiftly, he picked me up and carried me toward the deck. As he walked, I laid my head on his shoulder.

He lowered himself into a lounge chair on the deck, and sat me down beside him. He scooted across the lounge a little bit, and looked at my face. His lips started to quiver again.

"Go get a shirt, Ripp, and give me my hoodie back," he said as he pointed to the back door of the house.

He reached up to his chest and rubbed his dog tags.

"So, what happened? Slowly, Kace. Tell me slowly," he almost whispered as he spoke.

"Joth came home drunk. He wuth being an athhole. We argued about thome beer he was mithing, and he hit me. He knocked me on the floor and kicked me in the fathe. When I woke up, I got a thkillet and hit him in the head," I paused and took a slow breath.

"Hard," I smiled.

Shane shook his head from side to side.

"That motherfucker. He's alive, right?" he raised his eyebrows and nodded his head once.

I thought about what Josh looked like on the couch and how hard I hit him.

I shrugged my shoulders.

"Probably?" I said, wondering if he might be dead.

He laughed and patted my knee, "A skillet, huh? You did good."

The other man came through the back door and tossed Shane his hoodie. He was wearing a pull over hoodie that said "Gold's Gym" on the front.

"Ripp, this is Kace," Shane said as he leaned back and pointed my direction.

"Pleasure to meet you. Mike Ripton. Call me Ripp or Mike," he said as he held his massive hand in front of me.

I leaned forward and shook his hand.

"You're huge," I said.

"Ith he mean?" I whispered to Shane.

Shane laughed.

"She wants to know if you're mean, Ripp" he laughed over his shoulder.

"Ripp's like a pit bull puppy. He's a hell of a lot of fun until you piss him off." Shane chuckled.

Ripp slid a chair across the floor and sat in front of us with a plate of chicken and a bottle of beer.

"Water?" he asked as he handed me a bottle of water.

"Thank you," I responded as I reached for the water.

Quickly, he pulled the bottle of water close to his chest.

Holy shit, he's fast.

I turned and looked at Shane, surprised.

"I'll give you this water if you tell us what happened, and where that piece of shit is," he said.

"She already did," Shane said.

Ripp stood up, set down the plate, and handed me the water. He licked the barbeque sauce from his fingers and popped his neck.

"Let's go," he said as he wiped his hands on his shorts.

"Sit down, Ripp," Shane shook his head, "let her finish."

Ripp turned and walked back into the house.

"He's kind of a hot-head when he gets mad. Don't pay any attention to him. He's a great guy. He's a lot like me. He hates it when men mistreat women. He's not mad at you, okay?"

I nodded slowly.

"So," he leaned forward and looked at my mouth, "You have the tooth?" he asked.

I nodded and patted my pants pocket.

Ripp walked back onto the deck with something in his hand. He leaned over and handed the object to me.

"It's an icepack. Put it on your lips. Probably too late, but it won't hurt. It'll make 'em feel better," he smiled.

"Thanks Ripp," Shane said.

Ripp sat back down and grabbed his plate of chicken. I watched him as he devoured half a chicken in a matter of seconds. Being around two men who were caring, kind, and treated me with respect was different. I had never witnessed this type of care before. Not since I was sixteen, anyway. I continued to watch in amazement as Ripp ate chicken like an animal.

"Kace, you okay?" Shane asked as he patted my knee with his hand.

"Oh, yeah. Thorry. He eath a lot," I said as I nodded toward Ripp.

Shane turned and looked at Ripp. He shook his head and laughed, "Yeah. He has to feed the machine."

Ripp nodded, "We had a deal little girl. Tell your story."

I moved the icepack from my face and set it in my lap.

"Joth and I have been together for ten yearths. He threatenth me, thlapth me, and chokth me all the time. He beat me today for the lath time. I hit him in the head with a thkillet. Heeth uncontheeouth," I said toward Ripp.

I wiped my palms on my jeans and smiled at Shane. I wanted him to be proud of me.

Ripp licked the barbeque sauce from his hands and stood up from his chair. He looked at Shane and shook his head slowly.

"I think I understood her, but with her lips swollen and she's all busted up and missing a tooth, it's tough. What'd she say, Dekk?" he asked as he wiped his hands on his shorts.

"She said he beats her, chokes her, threatens her, and slaps her as a matter of normal occurrence. They've been together ten years. He kicked her teeth out today and it'll, according to her, be the last time,"

Shane paused, turned, and looked at me.

I nodded.

"She say she hit him with something?" He asked as he licked his fingers and walked closer to me.

"Oh, yeah. She hit him in the head with a skillet. Hard. Split his head open and he was unconscious when she left," Shane responded.

As I sat beside Shane, Ripp walked up to the chair we were sitting on and leaned over. Slowly, he reached toward my face and placed his cupped hand under my chin. Using his hand, he raised my chin up to take a closer look at my face. I moved the ice pack away from my mouth.

He squinted his eyes and gazed at Shane. He looked back at me and moved his hand away from my chin.

"What do you weigh, a hundred pounds?" Ripp asked incredulously.

"Thometimeth," I responded.

"Sometimes," Shane said.

"Dependth on what I eat," I said.

"Depends on what she…" Shane started to say.

"I can fucking understand her. It just takes me a minute," Ripp said angrily as he shook his head.

"He's not mad at you, babe. He's just mad," Shane said as he rubbed my thigh.

Shane stood up from the lounge chair and met Ripp's gaze.

"I'm gonna kill him, Dekk. The dead kind," Ripp said as pressed the knuckles of his right hand into his left palm.

"I'll take care of this," Shane said.

Ripp shook his head.

"Sorry, brother. Can't let that happen. I gotta leave you here with the girl. If something goes to shit, if the cops get called, I can't risk that. She *needs* you. Look at her. And I don't just mean *now*. Shit, Dekk. When you tell me stories about you two eating lunch…well, your fucking eyes light up. This little girl means the world to you. Let's let what happens between you two happen. If you're in jail, she's alone again. Hell, that fuck nugget might come back," he said.

Shane pulled his hood over his head and paced back and forth across the deck.

"I don't know, Ripp. It's *my* deal. It's *my* fight. I don't let people fight my fights for me," Shane said as he shoved his hands in his hoodie pockets.

"Listen to me, Dekk," Ripp turned toward Shane.

Shane stopped pacing and faced Ripp.

"You got *nobody*. You ain't got a dad, and you ain't got any family that I know of. I got two sisters and a mother and father. I never had a brother – until I met you. Always wanted one. You *need* to take care of this girl. Let her take care of you – she needs that too. This is about minimizing risk. I got this. You're in Texas, not Compton. This is how we do it here in the great state of Texas. We take care of our family. You're my family," he wrapped his arms around Shane and hugged him.

"Let me go with ya," Shane said as Ripp released him.

"No can do, bro. I told ya. I got this," Ripp responded as he wiped his hands on his shorts.

Shane shook his head and rubbed his hood into the sides of his face.

"Just don't kill him," Shane said.

"Can't make that promise, bro. We'll see how it goes," Ripp said as he walked toward the barbeque grill.

"Damn it, Ripp," Shane said softly, almost as if talking to himself.

"I ain't gonna do it right now. I need to eat," Ripp said as he grabbed a few more pieces of chicken from the platter which sat beside the grill.

He walked back toward his chair with a plate full of chicken. As he sat in the chair and started devouring another piece of chicken, he nudged his head toward the back door.

"Go inside Dekk and get her a piece of paper off my desk. And a pen. I need her to write down everything about this asshole she's willing to tell me. Everything," he said as he dropped a bone onto the plate.

As I watched him eat it dawned on me he was probably the biggest human being I had ever seen. I have never seen anyone, of any size, that was as muscular as he was. He was a boxer, like Shane, but he was huge. Without a doubt he would either beat Josh half to death or possibly even kill him.

After spending ten years with Josh, I realized a small part of me should feel sorrow for what might happen. Maybe I should feel a little compassion and want to prevent it from occurring.

I felt nothing.

I looked at him as he ate another piece of chicken. His head was cleanly shaven and he had hair on the tip of his chin. He was very tan, almost like he was Hispanic, but he was white. As he chewed, I could see the muscles in his neck and jaw flex.

"Is your head thmooth?" I asked.

I have no idea why I asked that.

He dropped the bone onto the plate and wiped his mouth with the back of his hand.

"Is my head smooth?" he chuckled, "smooth as butter. You wanna touch it, don't ya?"

My head bobbed up and down as of its own will.

"Well, get over here. And don't be dripping that cold ice pack on me when you're fingering my head," he laughed.

I stood up from my lounge chair and walked beside the chair he was sitting in. I stood and stared at his smooth head.

"Well, I can't put my head in your hand, Shorty. You're just going to have to reach over here and rub it. Take that ice pack off of your lips and let me see them," he said softly.

I pulled the ice pack from my mouth and smiled. He shook his head and chuckled.

"Well, I've seen a lot worse. You'll heal up just fine, you hear me?" he said as he leaned my direction.

I nodded my head. Slowly, I reached toward his head with my left hand. As I did, he raised his head closer to my hand. I touched it with my fingers. It felt soft and smooth, like my legs after I shave them. No stubble whatsoever.

"Don't get any wild ideas. I know it feels nice, and you look really good with that long blonde hair. Now go sit down before Dekkar comes out here and whips my ass again," he laughed.

"Again?" I asked.

"Yeah, again. He didn't tell you?" he asked.

I sat back down on the lounge chair and turned his direction, "Nope."

"Well, that's how we met. Crazy fucker rode his bike here from Compton. Got off of it, put on a set of gloves, and stepped into the ring. I stepped in with him. Biggest god damned mistake of my career. He's got the fastest hands I've ever seen. Powerful too. You wouldn't know it. Hell, he wears that fuckin' hoodie everywhere, covering up his body. He's probably the meanest son-of-a-bitch I've ever met. Anyway, maybe thirty seconds into the fight he hit me three times before I even knew it. Knocked me out cold. First time I've ever been on the mat," he picked up another piece of chicken and took a bite as he nodded his head once.

I thought about Shane fighting him. I imagined Shane knocking him out. I remembered how big Ripp was as he stood in the yard with his shirt off. I started to get uncomfortably warm. My pussy started to ache. I wanted Shane, and I wanted him bad. Josh and I had not had sex in almost three years. I desperately needed a man. I began to imagine Shane kissing me and undressing me as he did.

Oh God.

I crossed my legs again.

Bad idea.

I looked at Ripp as he pulled the meat from a chicken bone. I uncrossed my legs. *Oh God, I'm soaked.* Thinking of Shane got me really excited. I needed to go to the bathroom. As I pulled the icepack from my mouth, Shane walked out onto the deck.

"Ripp, I decided to let you do this. You're right, I want the girl. If it comes up again, or if he shows his face a second time, he's mine. Deal?" he asked.

He's talking about me!

I felt flush.

I want the girl.

"Deal," Ripp said as he dropped the last bone onto the plate.

I stood up, set the ice pack on the lounge, and reached up toward Shane's face with both hands. As I stood on my tip-toes, he leaned down and looked at me through his hood. I flipped the hood off of his head with my right hand. As it fell onto his shoulder, he slowly smiled.

"Kith me," I said as I stretched my face toward his.

My swollen lips met his, and he reached around me and picked me up. I felt his tongue against mine. I closed my eyes. I haven't been kissed in years, and I have *never* been kissed like that. Shane was right; everything he does, he does extremely well. As my feet dangled a foot above the floor of the deck, I felt warmth inside of me I had never felt. It was at that point I *knew*.

Shane Dekkar would always protect me.

RIPP

Laws are set in place as a set of rules and regulations to protect people who do not or are not breaking them from the few who do. It really doesn't matter where you live or what you believe in, for the most part all countries have the same laws to provide the same protection.

Don't steal, don't take advantage of people, don't harm people, and don't intimidate or threaten people. As a general matter of law, those rules sum it up just about everywhere. Every law falls within one of those categories, regardless of where you reside.

The punishment varies from country to country. Some countries cut the hands off of thieves. Others place them in jail. Even countries who may look at women as a substandard form of life do not allow them to be harmed or taken advantage of against their will. I know many women who have attempted to file charges against their boyfriends or husbands for abuse. Almost every occasion ended up with the woman filing charges a second time for a crime much worse - because the first occurrence went unpunished. A man who intimidates or beats a woman, generally speaking, does not want to be confronted by a man who is willing to stand up for the woman or her rights.

Men who abuse woman, without exception, are cowards.

I like to remind them of the fact that they're spineless. It satisfies me.

After we first met, Dekkar and I found this to be a common belief between us. A week or so after we met the first time, we ate lunch together. The conversation immediately went to our system of beliefs. His strongest belief was the fact women are not to be abused, ever - verbally, mentally, morally or physically. I believed the exact same thing. He was able to describe many circumstances when he became involved in an attempt to resolve a domestic issue which included a woman in need.

I was astonished. It was the one thing that brought us closer to each other - a similar belief in what we understood to be moral. Additionally, we both believed an outside influence often worked much better than filing a domestic violence charge with police.

Stepping in and resolving an issue with a man's abuse of a woman didn't necessarily *require* violence. It always depended on the circumstances. Violence breeds violence, and violence is never the ultimate answer. It is, however, a useful tool in *some* circumstances.

"Whoa!" Josh screamed as I walked into the living room of the house.

"How the fuck did you get in here? I'll call the cops," he yelled.

"Turn off that fucking television and shut the absolute fuck up," I said as I pulled the hood of my sweatshirt off of my head.

He sat and stared at me as if in shock. I reached down and picked up the remote control from the floor and turned off the television. As I did, he started to stand up.

"You aren't going to call anyone, you don't have a phone. Sit the fuck down. You and I are going to have a long talk," I said as I dangled Kace's set of keys from my fingertips.

He stood and stared at me as I walked across the living room and sat down in the chair beside the couch.

"This is *my* house…"

I interrupted him before he finished, "Say one more God damned word without me asking you a question. One fucking more, *just one*. I'll knock every tooth out of your mouth and wear 'em around my neck on a chain. Say something. *Anything*."

Silently, he slowly lowered himself onto the couch.

"That's it, just sit down. I need to talk to you while you're able to comprehend it. Later you'll be more liable to forget what I say," I said as I pointed to the couch.

He scrunched uncomfortably on the couch, burrowing a little deeper into the cushions.

"This is about Kace and what you did to her today. I talk, you listen. Understand?" I asked as I unzipped and took off the jacket I wore over my hoodie.

He nodded. His head had a knot on it about the size of a tangerine. I stood up and pulled my hoodie off over my head. Purposely, I didn't wear a shirt. I sat back down into the chair, laid the hoodie down, and flexed my biceps just to make sure he knew what may be coming later.

"I don't like you. People like you make me make me want to spend my life in prison for murdering them. The only thing preventing me from doing it is the fact that being in prison would keep me from finding another piece of shit like you and doing this all over again. Believe it or not, I *enjoy* this. The satisfaction I get from stopping you from abusing another woman is the same satisfaction most men get from fucking, multiplied by about ten. Remember, not a word unless I ask you," I rolled my shoulders and popped my neck.

He sat and stared.

"Now, when I start talking, you're naturally going to want to say something to defend yourself. I wouldn't advise that. If you do, I'm going to get up, come over there, and beat on you. Eventually, I'm going to do it anyway. If you try talking your way out of this, it's just going to make it last a really long time. If you keep your mouth shut, I'm going to sit here and just talk - at least for now. Understand?"

He nodded.

"Men who abuse women are fucking pussies. They're the lowest form of life that exists. Talking down to women, screaming at them, intimidating them, or physically harming them in any way is abuse. Abuse isn't going to be tolerated by me, ever," I took a slow breath and looked him over.

Talking to this asshole wasn't sitting very well with me. It was all I could do to look at this guy. Knowing eventually I was going to knock at least one of his teeth out was extremely satisfying.

"You've spent the last ten years intimidating Kace, and you're done. *Completely.* The shit that went on here this afternoon is the last of it. You'll never speak to her again for any reason. You will make no effort to contact her, ever. You will not approach her, call her, text her, or have any of your friends attempt to do so. Understand?" I asked as I rubbed my hands on the thighs of my jeans.

He nodded.

"No, I need verbal confirmation. *Do you understand*?" I asked.

"Yeah," he said.

"I'm not one of your punk friends. Don't talk to me like one. If you respond affirmatively, it better be a *yes*. Understand?" I pushed against my thighs with my hands and sat up straight.

94

"Yes?" he said with a confused look on his face.

Covered with sweat, he reached up and wiped his brow. As he wiped his hand on his jeans, the sweat beads began to re-form on his face.

"It's hot as fuck in here, what's the temperature set at? I asked.

He shrugged his shoulders and wiped his face again.

"Well, it's so fucking hot in here I'm un-goddamned-comfortable. Son-of-a-bitch that knot on your head looks painful. She got you good, didn't she?" I chuckled.

Lightly, he touched his swollen head with his fingertips. As his fingers touched the knot, he squinted and jerked his head backward.

"Okay, we're getting off track. I'm going to need some answers from you. Listen up. Are you ever going to try to talk to Kace again?" I asked.

"Well, I…" he started.

As he began to speak, I stood up, "Shut up. Obviously you didn't hear me or understand me."

"You said don't speak unless you asked me to," he said as he leaned back into the couch cushions.

I took a few steps toward him and stood directly in front of the couch, "Stand up."

He sat still and looked up at me as if confused on what to do. I reached down and got ahold of his hair and pulled him up from the couch.

"Holy shit, dude. God damn. I'm coming. Fuck," he said as I raised him off of the couch cushion by his hair.

"Shut the fuck up," I demanded as he stood directly in front of me, his hair in my left hand.

"When you choke Kace, this is what it feels like," I said as I grabbed his neck in my right hand.

I squeezed as hard as I could until his eyes rolled back and he began to go limp. I released the pressure on his neck. As I did, he began to cough and gasp for air. I pulled upward on his hair, forcing him to stand erect.

"Oh my fuckin' God," he coughed and sputtered as I continued pulling against his hair.

"And this is what it feels like when you slap her," I said as I reached back and slapped his face as hard as I could with my open right hand.

The slap knocked his head from my grasp. He fell to the floor, crying. I stood above him and with my left hand grabbed another fist full of his hair.

"Dude, that's fucking gross, your hair came out," I said as I brushed the hair from my hand onto the floor beside him.

"Get up, you pussy. Get up right now or I'm going to cut off your cock," I threatened, knowing I wouldn't touch his cock with a ten foot pole.

Slowly, he rose to his feet, rubbing his jaw the entire time.

"Being slapped hurts, don't it?" I asked.

He nodded his head slowly.

Whack!

I slapped him with my left hand. His legs wobbled.

Whack!

I slapped him with my right hand.

He began to stumble and fall to the floor.

I grabbed each of his shoulders in my hands and stabilized his stance.

"You alright to stand?" I asked as I let go of his shoulders.

He stood fairly erect, sobbing and rubbing his jaw.

"Brace yourself," I said.

"What? Brace…what?" he mumbled through his hands.

"I'm going to break a rib. You'll need to tighten up your stomach muscles. If you don't, you'll puke on me. If you puke on me, I may kill you. We've already discussed that. I don't *really* want to kill you," I said calmly.

"Dude, what the fuck…" he started to speak through his cupped hands.

Before he could finish speaking, I pushed him away from me. As he began to stumble backward, I unleashed a series of body punches to his mid-section. He began to fall backward. As he fell, I swung a ferocious right fist into his ribs and followed with an immediate left hook. I felt his ribs break under my knuckles.

Although I hadn't originally intended to do so, as his face began to slump forward, I swung a right uppercut. It just felt natural. The punch caught him right under the chin. The power of the punch lifted his feet from the floor and sent him reeling backward. While he attempted to remain on his feet, his legs turned to rubber and he collapsed to the floor.

Shit, knocked out twice in one day.

I kicked him lightly with my foot.

"Get up," I said as I kicked him again.

"Get up you piece of shit," I said as I kicked him a little harder.

He lay motionless on the floor.

I walked to the kitchen and grabbed a glass bowl from the kitchen countertop. I filled it with water and walked back into the living room. I pressed my foot into his stomach and poured the water directly onto his face. As the water hit his face, he began to sputter and tried to speak.

"Oh… my," he slowly held his stomach.

"God, I need an ambulance," he groaned as he rocked his head from side-to-side.

I pressed on his stomach with my foot. As I did, he began to cry.

"Please," he cried.

"Shut the fuck up. We're just getting started. I need to ask you some questions again. You have the attention span of a fucking gnat," I said as I carried the bowl to the chair and sat down.

"Now, you twat waffle, listen. Are you going to ever make any effort to contact Kace for any reason?" I asked.

Lying on the floor, he did his best to shake his head from side-to-side. As he did, I stood up and crossed my arms.

"No," he tried to scream. As he did, he winced in pain and held his ribs.

"You're not going to want to take too many deep breaths or scream. I felt about three of those things break. Broken ribs are a bitch. Just trying to breathe becomes so painful you'll want to die. That's why I broke 'em. So you'd remember I was here. Okay, where were we? Let's see. No contacting Kace. I'm glad you're a great learner," I laughed.

"And stop whining, I am not going to fucking call you an ambulance. You didn't call one for Kace, did you? You fucking scumbag, the more I talk about this, the more I *do* want to kill you," I complained.

He raised himself up onto his elbows and started crying out loud.

"You fucking punk. Shut up. Do you have any tools in here? In the house?" I asked.

Confused, he looked at me and squinted. I raised my hands in a defensive boxing posture and clenched my jaw. I took one step in his direction.

"Utility room," he said softly as he nodded his head toward the kitchen.

"Don't go anywhere," I laughed, knowing he probably couldn't even stand.

I walked into the utility room and found two tool boxes on the shelves above the washer and dryer. I opened one. It contained pliers, a hammer, wrenches, screwdrivers, electrical tape, and basic repair type tools. *Perfect.* I opened the other. It contained gardening tools and chemicals. I removed the pruning shears from the gardening box and placed them into the first tool box and closed the lid. I walked into the kitchen and opened drawers until I found dish rags and towels. I grabbed a few towels and stuck them in my back pocket.

As I walked into the living room, Josh was sitting against the couch on the floor.

"Nice selection of tools. I'll make this quick. Well, it'll be kind of quick. You're going to need to listen again," I said as I placed the tool box between the chair and the couch.

"Okay. I'm going to say this now, later it'd make no sense to you," I looked down at him and smiled.

He looked up confused.

"If you go to the hospital or the doctor, they're going to ask questions. You have a knot on your head that's six or so hours old. You have other fresh wounds. They'll want to know what happened. You *could* tell them about me coming here. If you choose to, my buddy will come find you. He makes me look like a real pussy. He'd probably go ahead and kill you, but do it really slow. If you have any great ideas or plans to get even or try anything, you might want to remember he knows you, and he hates you more than I do. I volunteered to come here – to save you from *him*," I pressed my index finger to my lips and thought.

"Okay, so yeah, probably no trips to the doctor. And Kace is not going to file charges against you for what you've done or what you did today. *This* is your punishment. It's just easier this way," I paused and turned away for a second.

"So, this might sound really bad at first, but I want you to think about it for a second before you answer. No rash decisions. I'm going to let you decide what we do next, okay?" I said softly as I turned around to face him.

Without speaking he nodded. I bent down and opened the tool box. I removed the hammer and the pruning shears, holding one in each hand.

"Okay, I'll let *you* pick. I can either cut the tip of your index finger off, or hit you in the mouth with this hammer and knock out a couple teeth. Which one sounds better?" I asked as I rotated the tools in my hands in front of him.

"Oh God. Please. I'm gonna throw up," he moaned.

"Well, if you have to you have to," I said.

"You're crazy. Seriously, you're crazy. *My finger?*" he complained as he held his ribs.

"Not your finger, just *part of it*. And crazy? No, let me tell you about crazy. Crazy? Crazy is you being the man in a relationship with a one hundred pound woman who only wants to be loved and cherished," I paused and shook my head.

"And beating her, intimidating her, and taking things from her just to control and manipulate her. Taking her phone, her Kindle, her freedom. Choking her. Not letting her see her parents. And beating her until she's down to the floor, and kicking her teeth out. Kicking a woman in the face after you beat her and she's lying on the floor. All to a fucking *girl*. Someone who trusts you, someone you're supposed to *protect*. You manipulative piece of fucking shit," the more I spoke the angrier I became.

I looked down at him as he sat against the front of the couch. I clenched my jaw and shook my head. *This motherfucker wants to call me crazy?* Without a second thought, I leaned forward and swung the hammer toward his mouth. Having never hit anyone in the mouth with a hammer, I didn't quite know what to expect. It felt like I was hitting a piece of wood, driving the hammer through it - splintering the wood. His teeth snapped off as soon as the hammer made contact with them.

I tossed the hammer behind me several feet and bent down to look at his face.

"Don't you dare get blood on my jeans," I snarled.

With his hands cupped over his mouth he screamed and cried. Rocking back and forth onto the front of the couch, he blubbered tears and spit blood. Blood ran down his arms and dripped from his elbows onto the floor.

"Move your fucking hands, let me see what kind of damage we're talking about," I said as I reached for his hands.

As tears ran from his eyes and blood dripped from his elbows, he cried and sobbed.

"Hands!" I screamed.

"Holy fuck. God damn. Now *that's* the way to knock out teeth, huh? Shit. There's maybe five or six of them fuckers gone. Get you a mouthful of these," I said as I smiled, exposing my gold tooth.

"You know, I'd have let you pick – either your mouth or your finger. You should have picked *one*. But God damn it. The more I talked about what you did to that poor girl, the madder it made me. And just looking at you is irritating as fuck," with the pruning shears still in my hand, I sat down beside him on the floor.

I reached over and grabbed his right wrist. As I pulled his hand toward my chest, he moaned. I've never had my teeth knocked out with a hammer, but I suspected he was in shock, semi-conscious from the beating, and incapable of speech due to losing the mouth full of teeth and the mangled lips. All he had left was crying, and he began to do a lot of that.

As he sat and sobbed, I pulled a towel from my back pocket and wrapped his hand in it, leaving only his index finger exposed. I squeezed his wrist and as I did, he attempted to close his hand into a fist.

"If you make a fist and make this difficult, I'll go get that tree saw from the utility room and cut your entire fucking hand off. And whatever I cut off, I'm taking with me. Hold still, God damn it," I said as I squeezed his wrist harder.

I moved my left hand from his wrist to his hand. As I squeezed his palm in my hand, I opened the shears and lightly squeezed his index finger in the razor sharp jaws. Not having ever cut the tip of anyone's index finger off either, I didn't know what to expect. I had pruned multiple bushes, and in hindsight, the branches - regardless of girth, were always easy to snip in two. Quickly, I squeezed the handle of the shears. As soon as I began to squeeze, he jerked his hand and screamed.

As he screamed, the tip of his finger fell into my lap. Blood immediately spurted from the stub of what was left of his finger. I covered his finger with the towel his hand was wrapped in. Simultaneously, he slobbered and sobbed loudly. As he pulled his hand to his chest and cried, I stood up.

"God damn, I ended up getting a lot more of that fucker in the shears than I wanted to. I'm really sorry, looks like I got more than an inch of that fucker. Well, at least it was quick," I said as I bent down and picked up what appeared to be no less than half of his finger.

I pulled another towel from my back pocket and wrapped his finger in it. I shoved the towel wrapped finger into the front pocket of my jeans. I grabbed my hoodie from the arm of the chair and put it on.

"Don't want to forget this," I smiled as I pulled it over my head.

I grabbed the electrical tape from the tool box, and turned to face him. I held the tape in the air so he could see it.

"Let me see that hand, I'll tape that dish towel to it really good so you don't make a bigger mess on this carpet. You've got blood, tears, and snot everywhere," I chuckled.

I reached down, pulled his hand away from his chest, and went around the circumference of the towel several times with electrical tape. I tossed the tape onto the couch cushion and shook my head as I watched him rocking back and forth holding his hand.

"I think my work is done here. Get some ice on that finger and mouth. You'll need to wrap those ribs. They're going to hurt longer than anything else. You can Google everything, there's great medical advice out there. And dude, I have no idea where your teeth went when I smacked you with that hammer. That happened really fast. You might have swallowed those fuckers. Now remember," I kicked his thigh with my foot.

With his eyes full of tears, sobbing, he looked up at me.

I held my index finger to my lips, "Shhhhhhh. Just between you and me."

He stared.

I kicked him again.

He nodded slowly.

I turned and walked toward the front door. As I did, I felt like I had actually accomplished something. The feeling, to me, was similar to winning a boxing match. I reached for the handle, inhaled a deep breath, and exhaled as I opened the door. I walked out onto the front porch, shut the door, and pulled the keys Kace gave me from my front pocket. I pushed the key into the lock and locked the front door.

Safety first.

SHANE

My father joined the military immediately following the first Gulf War, in 1993. My mother was around for a few years following his enlistment, from what my grandfather told me, but she left us not too long after he joined the military. At the time we lived in Oceanside, in southern California. I really don't remember much of my childhood - I was shuffled around quite a bit and I suspect it all became too confusing to remember.

When they flew the planes into the world trade center, my father was deployed to Iraq and Afghanistan. I moved to Compton and lived with my grandfather at the time of his first deployment. From his first tour until his death, he was never really around more than a month or so at a time. I lived with my grandfather until he died.

Having someone in my life who prevented me from spending all of my time alone has always been important. I suppose it would be important to everyone, but it's one thing which helps me feel as if I'm normal. From what I can remember of my childhood, I had always been somewhat of a loner, and never had a tremendous amount of friends. I've never really been shy, just slow to let people into my life. As long as I had someone to keep me company, I was satisfied. In the past, my father, grandfather, and a former girlfriend have filled the void in my life.

I always had a tremendous amount of respect for my father. Although I rarely saw him, he devoted his time, his career, and ultimately his life for the country and what he believed in. As a tribute to him, and as a matter of respect, I wore his dog tags with me everywhere I went. They had become somewhat of a good luck charm to me. In the boxing ring they are not allowed, and I have always had my trainer or manager hold them while I fought.

I realize I have tremendous natural talent as a boxer. I could never imagine trying to box without the dog tags accompanying me to a fight. To me, it was as if my father was there with me, looking over me, cheering me on and providing me with support. A father who was never able to be present through my childhood was now present for every match.

Fighting without any family to support me was difficult. I relied totally on the support of my dog tags to be my family. Being without them would put me in the ring naked and without any form of protection.

"Now listen, Shane. This guy is a beast. You've watched his films. You've seen what he can do. Watch his left cross. He'll catch you blind. If he ever connects that thing, you'll have one hell of a time recovering," Kelsey stood behind me as I worked the speed bag.

"Where we headed if we beat this guy, Shane?" he asked as he clapped his hands.

"Big ticket, boss," I responded without looking away from the bag.

"That's right, *the big ticket*. You'll be on that card with the championship fight. You'll be on god damned television. Pay television, Shane - not ESPN. You're one fight away from being a household name," Kelsey said as he clapped his hands.

"You amaze me, Shane. I have never seen a boxer that is such a natural. You act like you're eating fucking dinner or going for a walk in the park. You've got a heart of ice, and nerves of steel. Hell, you can hear every word I say while you're fighting. I've never seen that. I've yelled at boxers for a lifetime, and after a round is over, they have no idea what I said," he said as I continued to work the bag.

"It's your job to tell me what to do, boss. It's mine to do it. You can see what I can't," I said as I hit the speed bag one last time.

"How you feel?" he asked.

I nodded sharply.

"Better get out in the hallway, they're calling you out in five," the floor manager said through the doorway.

"How we fighting this guy?" Kelsey asked as I sat on the bench beside him.

"Southpaw, boss. Just like you said," I responded.

"That's right. Tonight you're a lefty. Let's go," he said as he laced up my gloves.

I looked down at the floor and said my prayer. As I stood up I pounded my gloves together and tapped my dog tags with each glove.

We stepped into the hallway and waited for the call. As soon a *Jimi Hendrix, Red House* began to play I started to walk toward the ring. As I approached the ring, I saw Ripp and Kace right where they said they'd be. I stopped at the edge of the ring and lowered my head. Kelsey reached toward my neck and slowly removed my dog tags.

"Give 'em to my girl, boss," I said.

He nodded.

"Get in the ring, Shane," Kelsey said as he nodded toward the ring.

"Hand her the tags, boss. I need to see it," I said.

Kace was half sitting, half standing, and obviously excited. Ripp stood beside her, clapping and whistling. As Kelsey handed her the dog tags, she made eye contact with me.

"Who?" I screamed her direction.

She pointed at her chest.

I nodded and stepped into the ring.

I closed my eyes and jogged in place. Blocking out everything was easy for me. I waited for them to call my name. I was ready.

"…red corner….Mace Maaaaad Dogggg Wilsonnnnnn" the announcer said.

"And. In the blue corner. Shane Shame on Deeeeeeekkaaaaar," I opened my eyes and stepped to the center of the ring.

I stared into the eyes of Wilson.

"Listen up. I gave you your instructions in the dressing rooms. Obey my commands at all times. When I say break, I want a clean break. In the event of a knock down, I'll direct you to a neutral corner. I want a clean fight. Protect yourselves at all times. Any questions?" the referee asked Wilson.

Wilson shook his head.

He turned his head to face me, "Any questions?" he asked.

"No sir," I responded.

"Touch 'em up," he said.

We touched gloves and headed to our corners.

"Remember what we talked about," Kelsey said sharply.

I bit my mouthpiece and nodded my head.

"This left handed son-of-a-bitch might try and lace ya, or butt ya, watch it. You know he's dirty, Shane," Kelsey reminded me.

I nodded my head.

Ding!

As I felt Kelsey slap my back, I jumped up and headed to the center of the ring.

Wilson met me in the center and began to circle to my left. After a few feeler punches, he started to peek-a-boo.

You wanna play peek-a-boo, motherfucker? I'll get those arms down.

I connected a few punches to his elbows, forearms, and lit him up with a series of body shots.

"Make him come to you," I heard Kelsey scream.

I tried a left hook, hoping for his liver. I caught an elbow, and he came back with a quick combination. His right jab caught me good, and glanced off to the left side of my face.

I stepped back and made him come to me.

As he stepped in and started on me, I heard Kelsey, *"Stay inside and counter, kid."*

Fucking Kelsey.

What have I told that old prick about calling me kid?

I threw a series of hooks and uppercuts. With my chin tucked and my head down, I noticed an opening. I have always been a master at counterpunching, and as soon as I saw it, I threw a right hook and a left uppercut. The uppercut caught the corner of his chin. He stumbled back and to his left.

Kelsey's screaming got louder. *"Stay inside, kid. Work that motherfucker! Counter!"*

Come here you big bastard. Let me see that chin. Let me see it, just once. That's all I need.

I worked his body and pummeled his arms with several flurries of punches. He was attempting to tire me. Obviously he didn't know much about me. I don't tire. Ever. I could easily do this all night. I worked against his arms and tried to get him to open up.

He countered with a series of jabs and a few hooks that caught my upper arms and shoulder. Although I saw the punches and felt my body move, the impact wasn't felt. When I fight, for the most part, I go numb.

"Left hook, kid. Get that left in there, God damnit," Kelsey screamed.

If that cocksucker calls me kid again...

I felt Kelsey's hand hitting the mat.

We're down to seconds.

I pushed him off, threw a right uppercut, and barely missed his chin.

Ding!

I found my corner and stepped to it.

"God damn it. You got to stay inside with this guy. You're too quick not to stay inside and counter this big bastard. You got him with that inside work, kid. Fifteen more seconds in that round and he would have been in trouble. He holds his right elbow tight. You'll get him with that left hook. Use it. Use it, God damn it," Kelsey screamed.

"Remember that guy in San Antonio last year? Tate?" he asked.

I nodded.

"He's fighting just like him. If he comes out in this round like he did in the last, stay inside and get him on the break. You're a damn site quicker than he is, kid," he bellowed.

As the bell rang, I scowled at Kelsey for calling me *kid,* jumped up and headed for Wilson.

As we met, I was immediately introduced to a series of his quick jabs. He did have fast hands, but his power was what worried me.

I followed him close, and the peek-a-boo bullshit started again.

You cock sucker, you trying to lure me? What have you got? What's your plan?

I got inside and worked his body and arms. It didn't seem to faze him at all. I continued to work his arms, knowing sooner or later he'd either lower his arms - exposing that chin - or try and punch his way out. If he tried to punch his way out, I'd left hook his ass into next fucking week.

I worked his right arm hard with my left hook.

My left's just as strong as my right you big prick. Did you like that? Hurt, didn't it?

I swung a left hook as hard as I could. The punch caught him right above the elbow. He winced from the impact.

How'd that feel?

I got him with a series of rights, and a left that caught his right elbow, shoving it into his ribs. He face contorted.

Oh. Did that hurt ya?

I threw two more quick lefts to his body, just below the elbow, followed up by a quick combination to his face. Instinctively, it caused him to raise his arms and try and fight his way out. As he raised his arms, I absolutely unleashed on his torso. Seven or eight quick punches to his mid-section before he got his arms down, and he looked like he'd seen a ghost.

Didn't know I was that fast, did ya, big boy?

He threw a right jab and missed. I countered with a right uppercut and a left hook. The left hook caught his lower abdomen.

He tucked his elbows and winced.

Well, big boy, I either got a rib, or your liver's hurtin'. Sorry, but this is gonna hurt like a mother fucker.

I immediately stepped in and worked his body with a quick

combination, followed by a left uppercut. The uppercut caught him on the right side of the face – a glancing blow. As his head turned left, his right elbow came up.

"Body, kid. Body. Open him up, kid. Body!" I head Kelsey scream.

Where's that bottom rib, Wilson? Where is it? I want it. I need it.

I went back to the body. As he lowered his arms to protect his body, I threw a few quick jabs to his face.

Better get those arms up. Protect that ugly face of yours. Remember what happened last time? I'm too fast for ya. Get 'em up. I want that right side. I need me a rib.

There have been several times in my career when I felt like I could see a few seconds into the future. For those moments, I have always been grateful. I do realize I don't *really* see into the future, but it sure seemed like it. In a boxing match, knowing what's next is a huge plus. This was one of those times everything happened slowly. I felt as if I had an hour to plan the series of punches I eventually unleashed.

As he raised his arms, Kelsey started to scream.

"Get those ribs, kid. Body! Body! Body! His liver, God damn it, his liver! Body!" Kelsey screamed.

His arms came up.

Huge mistake, Wilson.

As he raised his arms, a right hook to his left side opened up his right side. A solid left hook caught him under his ribcage perfectly. His face distorted in pain. His elbows came down, exposing his chin.

Please Lord, forgive me for what I am about to do.

A quick right jab glanced off of his ear, causing him to raise his head. I threw a left uppercut with every ounce of my being. The left impacted his chin solid, lifting his head sharply. He was immediately unconscious. The unnecessary right cross missed his face as he began to fall to the mat like he was dead.

Time stood still.

His body collapsed to the mat. I stood over him. I wanted to see his eyes.

The referee stepped in front of me and pointed. I went to the neutral corner and paced back and forth.

Come on, get up. Get up. Get up.

The referee waved his arms. This fight was over.

I heard Ripp scream. *Shane motherfucking Dekkar.*

I waited. *Get up, you big fucker. You can do it.*

I saw Kelsey out of the corner of my eye. Wilson opened his eyes and began to sit up.

Thank you, Lord.

I turned and faced Kelsey. He was crying. He rubbed his eyes and opened his arms.

"We made it kid," He said as he hugged me.

I pulled my face away from him and smiled. He pulled my mouthpiece.

"Stop calling me kid, you old prick," I said.

"Boy he underestimated you with that peek-a-boo shit, didn't he," Kelsey laughed.

I nodded.

Kace and Ripp stepped into the ring and rushed toward us.

As Kace smiled, I remembered what she looked like without her tooth. Her now repaired teeth were perfect. I smiled in return.

"That was exciting, I'm hungry," she blurted as she reached into her pocket.

I placed my gloves on each side of her shoulders and held her still. As I bent my knees and lowered my head, she placed my dog tags over my head and onto my neck. As I started to speak, I heard the announcer.

"At 2:37 of the second, by knockout, *the winner*….Shane Shame on Dekkar…"

I turned and raised my hands. I walked toward Wilson and patted him on the back.

"Great fight, Wilson," I said as I looked him in the eye.

"You got hands, kid," he said as he patted my shoulder.

I nodded and turned toward Kace and Ripp. As I walked toward Kace, I could see she had settled down and wasn't quite as nervous.

"You okay?" I asked.

She nodded, "What were you going to say?" she asked.

I bent my knees again, lowering my face close to hers.

"Kith me," I chuckled.

As our lips parted I looked at her beautiful face. I looked up at Ripp, who stood beside her with his hand on my shoulder. Kelsey stood behind Ripp, wiping tears from his eyes as he talked to Joe. I looked toward Kace again. As she looked up at me and smiled, I realized *this* was my family.

And the ring was my home.

And I smiled.

KACE

The difference between wanting someone to love you and actually *being* loved is the difference between black and white. I suppose I could have lived the rest of my life thinking I was being loved; but now that I actually had it, I knew what I had in the past was nothing more than some fucked up form of affection.

Shane and I had been seeing each other for six weeks. In some respects, I felt like I had forced myself into his life. In others, it seemed as if I were invited. After the incident with Josh, I moved in with Shane; in his spare bedroom. It pleased him to look over me and feel like he was protecting me from anything or anyone who might hurt me.

When I thought of the month or so Shane and I spent together before I left Josh, and the six weeks which had followed, it seemed to me like two years of time had passed. I knew more about Shane in this period of time than I ever knew about Josh. Shane was quiet to everyone except Ripp and me. To me, he could talk for hours on end. I liked it when Shane talked to me, it stood as proof he cared about what I thought, wanted, or expected in life.

Shane had not told me he loved me, but I knew in some sense he did. I could feel it. He wasn't broken inside like a lot of people are who do not have family, he was just shy. And although he was shy, he was still able to love and be loved. More than anything, I wanted Shane to love me. I wanted to be his, and I wanted him to be mine.

"I couldn't decide if I liked the five miles better than three or not," he said as he collapsed on the couch.

I walked over and sat at the edge of the couch beside him.

"Well, you ought to know by now, we've been running the five for a month and a half," I said as I pressed my hands into his shirt.

"Well, there are things about it I like, and things I don't. I like the amount of time it takes, but I don't like the speed we run. I'm used to running faster," he said as he sat up.

"Everything you do is a competition. In your head, you compete with yourself," I said as I slipped my hands under his shirt and felt his stomach muscles.

"I suppose so. I'm just used to running a mile in a little less than six minutes. We don't run that fast. You run like a girl," he chuckled.

"You can't run five as fast as you run three, and I *am* a girl," I laughed as I pushed him backward onto the couch.

As he fell, he pulled me with him. I landed face first on his chest, and he wrapped his arms around me. I pressed my face into his massive chest, smelling his shirt as I buried my nose in between the muscles of his chest.

"I love how you smell when you get out of the shower," I said as I raised my face from his chest.

"Who's the most beautiful woman in the world?" he whispered.

I smiled.

"Who?" he whispered as a smile formed on his face.

I love it when he does this.

I pointed to my chest.

"That's right," he responded.

His hands massaged my back as I looked into his eyes. His eyes were the strangest color of grey. They were almost a translucent grey/blue. His eyes alone caused me to feel as if I was powerless against him. Combining his personality, sensitive nature, shy quiet demeanor, and the fact that he was muscle from head to toe was enough to push me over the edge.

Every time.

He could take advantage of me at any point in time he preferred; the fact he didn't made me admire and hate him both. I pushed my hands against his chest and raised my body from his. I looked down at his torso and chest. His tight tank top hugged his muscled torso.

This is freaking ridiculous.

"Why don't we ever go any further than this, Shane?" I asked as I admired his body.

He raised his hands to his face and covered his cheeks and eyes with his palms. As he rubbed his face, I grabbed his wrists and pulled his hands free and pressed them onto my shoulders. I wanted so desperately to place them on my chest, but I didn't want to make him uncomfortable.

He squinted his eyes and cocked his head to the side, "I don't want to take advantage of you."

"We've talked about this. Please, take advantage of me. I'm begging you," I laughed.

He smiled and rolled his eyes.

"It's not taking advantage of me if I want you to do it," I said as I held his wrists.

"It is if you're not ready," he responded as he squeezed my shoulders lightly.

"I'm ready," I said.

"I don't think so," he tilted his head and responded.

"Why?"

"Because it hasn't been *that* long. It's been seven weeks. That's it. A codependent woman will attach herself to the first man who presents himself after she gets out of a relationship. I don't want to be your man out of a feeling of necessity. I want to be your man out of feelings of deep desire," he said as he began to sit up.

I pushed against his chest, forcing him back to his laying position on the couch. I liked that he let me do silly things to him. As strong as he was, he could keep me from even making him move at all, but he played with me. He let me push him around and goof with him. He knew just how to act and what to do to make me feel at ease, and he never made me feel out of place or uncomfortable.

"Lay down," I said, pointing to his chest with my index finger.

"Yes ma'am," he responded as he leaned back onto the couch cushions.

"We're going to talk," I said.

"Talk. Alright. Get busy," he chuckled.

"Do you want to make me happy?" I asked.

"Absolutely," he responded.

"Let's make progress in this thing we have," I said.

"This thing…" his voice faded as he raised his eyebrows.

"Yes. I don't know what to call it. *This thing*. Let's go one step further. I want that," I smiled.

"One step," he responded with a smirk on his face.

I nodded.

He slid his hands from my shoulders to behind my neck, and slowly pulled my face to his. As his lips parted, I pressed my face hard against his. Kissing Shane was something I could do forever. He once told me everything he did he was great at, and kissing was no exception.

I closed my eyes and held his head in my hands. With our tongues intertwined and our wet lips massaging each other, I got lost in the feeling. Thoughts of the men in my erotica novels ran through my head. I opened my eyes and raised my face from his.

"I want you," I said, my voice filled with emotion.

"You *have* me," he responded as he wiped his lips with the back of his hand.

"No, I *want* you," I said.

"Kace, you have me - as much as I'm willing to give. I'm yours. You have all you can get. There is no more," he said as he started to sit up.

Frustrated, I pushed myself toward the other end of the couch and sat between his legs.

"Don't get angry, babe. Everything I do, I do for what I believe is best for you. I don't want to hurt you. I don't want anything to develop in this relationship because you're vulnerable," he said softly as he sat up.

He ran his fingers through my hair and moved it behind my ear.

"I like seeing your face, Kace. You're beautiful. Sex can be a manner of *expressing* one's love, but by no means is it a method of *measuring* the love one has for you," he ran his fingers through my hair and smiled.

"Sex is all we have left, Kace. Don't look at it as a form of verification or validity to confirm how I feel about you. The fact we're here together is validity in itself," he moved closer to me and kissed my forehead.

I wrapped my arms around him, feeling selfish as I did so. He was right. I didn't *need* to have sex with him to prove anything. I *wanted* to have sex with him because I wanted to. I hadn't had sex for almost four years, and I wanted Shane to fuck me until I couldn't walk. The fact he held this one act in reserve proved to me he cared more about me than I could ever expect anyone else to.

I was incapable of recalling what sex felt like. I relied solely on the descriptions in the books I read for the memories associated with sex. My memories were false, and they were the scenes from the many books on my Kindle. I lived vicariously through the heroines in my books, and made love to my book boyfriends.

"Okay. I understand better now. It's just hard," I admitted as I moved my head closer to his hand.

This man made it difficult for me to do anything but want more. To have someone who was built the way he was one thing in and of itself. His body clearly defied the laws of everything which was human and masculine. He had a small waist and abs that looked as if constructed of a flesh washboard. A massive chest twice as wide as his waist. His arms had muscles along the side of muscles. And he didn't care. He didn't flaunt it. He wore a hoodie in the summertime to cover his body, not exposing it for all to see.

He was intelligent. He didn't speak in a manner I would have expected a boxer to speak. He often thought for some time before he committed to answering a question. When he did answer, be it immediate or after some thought, his answers were clear, concise and well defined.

He was kind, compassionate, considerate, romantic, loving, caring and loyal. For me this combination was proving to be far more than I could take. An alpha male who could destroy a man in a moment for any number of reasons contrary to what he held precious to his system of beliefs.

Yet.

He held a woman close to his chest and made her feel as if she was the most precious person on this earth, as if she had no reason to fear anything when she was in his presence.

Shane Dekkar. A man to define what all men should desire to become.

Perfection, defined.

Perfection is defined in the mind as it sees what stands before it. We compare what it is we now see to what we have seen in the past. This comparison is only based on what experiences we have, and what we have exposed ourselves to. I have had minimal exposure in life, but I am not a fool nor am I foolish. Shane Dekkar, to me, is perfect. I could spend a lifetime exposing myself to the offerings of life, and this would not change. It is not an opinion, it is a fact.

His fingers continued to rake through my hair.

"I'll give you a lifetime to stop that," I whispered as I closed my eyes.

"I'll never stop," he whispered.

"Promise," I asked as I opened my eyes.

Softly, he pushed me onto my back and crawled on top of me. His hands quickly moved into my hair, his fingers raking through it as the massaged my scalp. I closed my eyes again.

"Open your eyes, babe," he whispered.

I opened my eyes.

"Do you understand how I feel about you?" he asked, his eyes filled with passion.

"Tell me," I responded as I closed my eyes.

I relaxed as he massaged my scalp with his fingers. He lowered his chest to mine and softly laid his body against me. He positioned his head beside mine and began to whisper in my ear. His warm breath made me shiver as he began to speak.

"Kace, I could spend the rest of my life happy with you, I am certain. I have no reason to believe otherwise. And although I suspect you feel the same way, I do not believe you are able to make a decision regarding a relationship with anyone right now and it be one hundred percent heartfelt, considering what you have been through for the last ten years," as he paused, I started to speak

"Shhhh," he said into my ear.

"If you feel the way I suspect you feel, the end result will be the same regardless of when we make the decision to take the next step. It is very important to me that the decision be made by what your *heart* desires, and not what you *think* you want. Almost daily, I wish we would have met by different circumstances," his breath on my neck made me smile a slow smile.

With my eyes still closed tightly, I whispered, "Why different?"

"Well, because. I imagine part, and only part of what you feel – you feel because you believe I *saved* you. I don't want you to desire me for that reason. I want you to desire me because of *who* I am, and what we have to offer each other for a lifetime, not for this moment," he kissed my neck as he finished speaking.

"So how do you know when it's time?" I could feel his heart beating against my chest.

"I'll just know, I imagine," he responded as his hand touched the side of my face.

"Open your mouth," he whispered.

My eyes still closed, I slowly parted my lips.

"Stick out your tongue," he said as he kissed my chin.

I pushed my tongue past my lips.

As his lips encompassed my tongue, I opened my eyes. His left hand moved from my hair to the side of my face. His hands lightly touching each of my cheeks, we continued to kiss. As I studied his eyes, I began to ache for more. I wanted this man with all I had within me. I wanted to feel him inside of me. I wanted to become one – to share and experience each other's bodies in the way love was defined.

Slowly, he raised his head, kissing my lips as he did so. He moved his hands from my face to my hips. Using the tips of his fingers he lightly lifted my shirt from my shorts, and slid his hands inside my shirt. As they moved across my stomach toward my chest, my breathing stuttered.

Please, please...take me, Shane. Oh God, Squeeze my...

His hands moved between my breasts and pushed flat against my chest. I could feel his pinky fingers against the inside of my breasts.

"Do you feel that?" he asked.

I felt my heart begin to race. My pussy became immediately soaked. This was embarrassing. Exciting, but embarrassing. I felt uncomfortably wet. No, I was soaked.

"What?" it took all I had to mutter that one word.

"Your heart?" he asked softly. His eyes closed as he spoke.

I blinked my eyes, focusing on the feeling of his hands against my breasts. "Yes," I sighed.

"I want to warn you, Kace. I already told you once, when we first met. But remember what I'm telling you today - mark my words, I'm coming for this. *Your heart.* Be prepared, because I intend to make it mine. *I'm coming for your heart, Kace,*" he whispered as his hands pushed softly against my chest.

It's already yours, Shane.
When the time comes, you'll know it.

SHANE

"When's Shorty showin' up?" Ripp asked as he tossed the chicken on the grill.

"Any time, but she said not to wait," I responded.

"Mike Ripton waits for no man. Or woman," he laughed.

"How much fucking chicken you got, Ripp?"

"Three of em. Shit Dekk, I'll eat one, she'll eat a piece, you'll damn near eat one. That leaves a few pieces to snack on," he said as he continued to load the grill with chicken.

I thought about it and nodded my head, affirming Ripp's chicken count.

"So, we're working into the end of summer, you gonna get them boots before they're gone?" he laughed as he closed the grill.

I looked down at my boots. Seeing them from this distance, they didn't look so bad - as long as I looked straight down at the tops of them. The sides and bottom were a different story.

"I'll never understand ya, Dekk. Weird fucker, you're probably the only mother fucker in Austin wearing Levi's and boots today," he chuckled as he sat down on the lounge chair.

"Probably," I said as I sat down on the lounge beside him.

"So, I never asked. Your girl drink?" he asked.

125

I shrugged my shoulders.

"You know, I admire you for not. She ain't drank here yet. She's been here for eight or nine Saturdays in a row, hasn't yet. I didn't know if she did when you guys went out," he said as he took a drink from his bottle of beer.

"Hasn't yet," I responded.

"Suppose that's good. I don't know where you find all the inspiration. But if she doesn't drink, hell, it'll be easy for you to keep up the good work," he laughed as he finished his beer.

"At least the Ultra's won't make me fat," Ripp said as he slapped his hand against his stomach.

"Obviously not," I said.

"What ya sayin' Dekk?" he asked.

"Just said it," I responded.

"I drink too much?" he asked.

"Didn't say that," I said.

"What *are* ya sayin?" he asked.

"Calories are calories," I said.

"95 a bottle. That's it. Hell, I drink a dozen of these fuckers, it ain't gonna hurt me. That's 1200 calories. So, no big deal. I bet I only drink five or six anyway," he said.

"1140. But yeah, 95 calories isn't many. You sure about that?" I asked.

"Fucking smart-ass. The Ultra's haven't got much, but damn they taste like it. Want one?" he chuckled.

"No, I'll stick with this," I said as I leaned over and grabbed my half-full glass of water from the table at the corner of the deck.

"I'm going in for some ice, need anything?" I asked as I stood up from my chair.

"No, I'm golden," Ripp said as he stood up.

I've enjoyed Ripp's routine of cooking chicken on Saturdays. It gave me something to look forward to. I've always liked routines, and had become almost reliant on the processes I had in place. When they don't happen for some reason, I feel deprived. I walked into the kitchen and opened the freezer. As I looked into it, I realized that he'd dumped all of the ice I had purchased into his beer cooler.

I reached to the back of the freezer to grab the plastic ice trays. A small plastic Zip-Loc style bag was lying on top of the ice trays. As I picked it up to move it, I realized what it contained.

"Ripp, you sick fucker," I screamed, knowing he couldn't hear me.

I tossed the bag to the side and pulled the tray from the freezer. I dumped half of the cubes into my cup and re-filled the tray and my glass with water. I slammed the freezer door, and walked back outside to the deck.

"Ripp, you sick fuck," I said as I closed the door behind me.

"What's up, Dekk?" he said over his shoulder as he moved the chicken around on the grill.

"Well, I noticed you used all the ice I bought for one," I began.

"What's sick about that?" he chuckled as he closed the lid to the grill.

"Well, nothing. But it was all gone. So I grabbed an ice tray. Well, I started to. There was a Zip-Lock bag on top of the ice, so I grabbed it to move it and…" I paused to see what he had to say.

"And…?" he asked.

"Well? The Zip-Lock bag. What the fuck, Ripp?" I asked.

He shrugged his shoulders, "Dude, I got nothing."

"The finger, Ripp. It had a finger in it," I mumbled as I sat down.

"Oh shit, I forgot about that little fucker. It's been in there for a bit. Let's get it outta there and look at it," he said as he wiped his hands on his shorts.

"Dude, I just saw it. I don't want to see it *again*," I complained.

"Well, fuck. I probably ought to get rid of it. Maybe the garbage disposal?' he asked.

"Hell, I don't know. It's kind of small," I responded.

"Yeah, but it's frozen. So basically it's like a piece of ice. It ought to just get ground up and melt in there, huh?" he asked.

"No. Fuck Ripp, it's *meat*," I responded.

He nodded his head slowly, "Yeah, suppose so. Meat and a little piece of bone."

"Alright, I'm done talking about it," I said as I rubbed my stomach and made a face like I'd eaten something rotten.

"You beat people half to death, and knock out every son of a bitch under the sun, and you wanna get sick over a little finger. Shit, it ain't no bigger'n a Vienna sausage," he laughed.

"I'm done with the finger talk," I said as I waved my hands in front of my stomach.

"Well, I need to do something with it before your girl finds it," he said.

"Yeah, no shit. Go do *something* with it," I begged.

He walked past me and into the house. In a matter of seconds, he walked back onto the deck. As he shut the door, I turned his direction.

"Well?" I asked.

He held up the finger tip, grasping it between his thumb and forefinger.

"What the fuck are you doing?" I asked.

He opened the lid to the grill and looked inside.

"Ripp, don't!" I screamed and I started to stand up from the lounge.

"Well fuck, it won't fit. Come here and look at this. Little fucker's too small to cook on here. It'll fall between the little metal bars. Shit. I was just gonna cook it as a joke," he said as he turned and gave me a disgruntled look.

Still holding the finger in his hand, he closed the lid to the grill. We both turned to the left side of the deck as we heard the gate open. Kace walked through the gate wearing a floral print sun dress. Our eyes widened as we turned and stared at each other.

"Hey," Kace said as she stepped toward the deck.

We both simultaneously turned toward the open gate. A tall blonde wearing jean shorts and a sleeveless black shirt followed Kace into the yard. They couldn't have shown up at a worse time, considering the fact we hadn't resolved the finger issue yet. I looked at Ripp and scrunched my brow.

"*Do something with it*," I whispered.

As he noticed the other girl, he quickly shoved the finger into the pocket of his Khaki cargo shorts.

"Hope you don't mind. I brought my friend," Kace asked as she stepped onto the deck.

"Not at all. I'm glad you did," I responded as I turned and looked at Ripp.

As they both stepped onto the deck, Ripp raised his eyebrows and wiped his hands on his shorts.

"Hi. I'm Mike. Mike Ripton. You can call me Ripp, everyone else does," he said as he walked toward her with his hand held out in front of him.

"I'm Olivia. You can call me Liv. Everyone else does," she chuckled as she shook Ripp's hand.

I hugged Kace as Ripp shook her hand. As I kissed her, Liv turned our direction. I reached around Kace's side and held my hand out.

"Hi, I'm Shane," I said.

"Yeah, Kace told me about you," she said as she shook my hand.

"Hope you like chicken," Ripp said.

"Love it," Liv responded as she walked toward the grill.

"Uhhm. Want an Ultra?" Ripp asked as he pointed to the beer cooler.

"Yeah, sure. I mean, as long as you have enough," she responded.

"I always have enough," he laughed as he leaned toward the cooler and opened the lid.

Kace squeezed me tight and buried her face in my hoodie.

"Hey Shorty," Ripp said as he waved at Kace.

Without looking, her face buried in my hoodie, Kace raised her hand from my back and waved at Ripp.

"She's nice," I whispered into Kace's ear.

"I told her about Ripp on the way here. She's the one I told you who works at the coffee shop by the deli," Kace whispered.

"Aaahhh," I responded as I turned toward Ripp. He and Liv were talking as he poked at the chicken with the tongs.

"Go grab a platter and stuff, Dekk," Ripp said as he stood at the grill talking to Liv.

"C'mon, babe. Let's go inside," I said as I motioned toward the door.

"So, she's the girl from the coffee shop on the corner?" I asked as I looked for a platter and plates.

"Uh huh. She's the one I've been talking to you for the last few months about," she paused and smiled.

"Well, you know," she shrugged.

"Okay, I was thinking so. She's single?" I asked.

"Uh huh. Yeah. Her boyfriend was the douche. I told you about him. They broke up a month ago. Something like that," she responded as I handed her some plates from the cupboard.

I grabbed a large platter, silverware, and a roll of paper towels. With my arms full, I leaned toward Kace and kissed her. As we kissed, she set the plates on the countertop and wrapped her arms around me.

"I like doing this with you, Shane. Cooking. Eating. Being a part of your life beyond just living together. I like this. It's. It's, well. It's like we're a real couple. I like this," she said as our lips parted.

"I like it too," I said as I adjusted the paper towels under my arm.

"I want this. I want this forever," she said as she picked up the plates.

"I do too," I responded as I started walking toward the door.

"Then let's do it. Let's take that step, Shane. I'm ready," she said.

"It's not a contest, babe. It's life. There's no time limit. If I'm truly what you think you want, need, and desire it'll happen sooner or later. I'm not going anywhere. And you'll wait as long as you have to. I am not going to do this in any manner I'm not comfortable with," I said as I held the door handle in my hand.

"Well, I'm ready," She smiled.

"Noted," I said as I opened the door.

As we walked out onto the deck, Liv and Ripp were sitting on the lounge chair together laughing. Each of them had a beer, and Ripp was trying to catch his breath from laughing.

"Looks like they're having fun," I whispered to Kace.

"Oh my God, Kace. He's funny," Liv said as she nodded her head toward Ripp.

"He *can* be," Kace laughed.

"No, he *is,*" Liv stated, still laughing.

"I was just telling her about your boots," Ripp laughed.

I raised one eyebrow and turned toward Ripp as I set the plates and silverware down on the table.

"Well, it's true," he said.

"Let me see the bottoms of them," she asked.

I shook my head and turned up the sole of my boot so she could see the holes. As she leaned over and looked, she gasped.

"Oh my God. Those are awful. You were so right," she laughed as she slapped Ripp's leg.

I turned toward Kace and rolled my eyes. As she set the plates down on the table, I sat on the edge of the lounge chair. Kace sat down beside me and leaned over, resting her head on my shoulder. As I wrapped my right arm around her, Ripp stood up and walked toward the grill.

"So, what's with the hoodie?" Liv asked quizzically.

"What about it?" I responded.

"Well, it's almost a hundred degrees. You're wearing a hoodie, boots, and jeans. Don't you feel out of place?" she asked as she motioned to Ripp and Kace.

I raised my eyebrows, looked at Ripp and Kace, then turned back to face Liv, "No. I don't."

"So, why wear it in the summer?"

"Habit I suppose."

"It's hot out here," she said as she fanned her face with her hand.

"Not too bad," I responded.

"Is there a reason?" she asked.

I thought about her question. I had worn a hoodie every day since as long as I could remember. It had become somewhat of a trademark. As much as I tried to recall, I didn't really know what started it. Going without one now would make me feel naked. I doubted if I could make it a day without having a hoodie on or available to put on.

"I don't know. Again, I suppose it's habit."

"He always wears one," Kace said as she lifted her head from my shoulder.

"I'm not trying to be mean, it just seems odd," Liv said as she stood from the lounge.

"I know two things for sure. Dekk's one weird fucker. And this chicken's done," Ripp said.

Liv grabbed the platter, walked to the grill, and stood behind Ripp. Ripp's back was about twice as wide as hers. Seeing her stand beside him put them both in perspective regarding size. Ripp was huge and she was exceptionally thin. She reached around Ripp and held the platter at his side.

"Thanks, Liv," Ripp said as he grabbed the platter.

I looked down at Kace's. She was smiling as she watched Ripp and Liv. I leaned over and kissed her forehead as she admired them. As she turned her head and looked up at me, I kissed her.

"They're cute," she silently mouthed the words.

I blinked my eyes and nodded. She leaned her head against my bicep as she rubbed my thigh. Almost immediately, I began to become aroused. I shifted my left leg and kicked it up on the lounge. *No help.* I raised my right leg and leaned into the lounge. *Damn it.* Kace shifted beside me lowered her head onto my shoulder, and began rubbing my thigh again. As she did, she could feel me hardening. Her hand moved to encompass my now swollen cock.

She turned her head and softly whispered into my ear as she squeezed my cock in her hand, "I want this."

She turned, looked at Ripp and Liv for a short moment, and turned to face me.

"I want it," she whispered.

I closed my eyes.

She squeezed harder as she stroked her hand back and forth along the bulge in my jeans.

I kicked my legs over the other side of the chair and picked her up in my arms. Her face was filled with surprise as I swept her from the lounge and into my arms. Now standing on the other side of the lounge and holding her in my arms, she looked up at me and smiled.

"Ripp, we're going in the house for a minute," I sighed.

Ripp looked up from the grill, "Uhhhm. Alright."

Still holding Kace in my arms, I leaned toward the door and grabbed the handle. As I opened the door, Kace looked up at me and smiled. I walked into the living room and slowly lowered her onto the couch. As she lay on the couch, I knelt on the floor beside her and lowered my head alongside her hips.

"I want you…" she began to say as she kicked her sandals to the floor.

I pressed my finger to her lips.

"Shhhh." I said.

"Remember what I told you? About me being good at everything that I do?" I asked as I held my finger over her lips.

She nodded her head and sighed.

"I want you to listen to me, Kace. Listen and try to be quiet. Focus on listening and feeling," I said as I slid the bottom of her dress up to her hips.

I removed my hoodie and shirt and tossed them over the arm of the couch. I lowered my chin to the inside of her bare thighs, looking up at her eyes as I did. As I reached up and slowly pulled her panties down her thighs, she sighed softly. I tossed her thong on the couch beside her, reached inside her dress, and placed my hands against her waist. I pressed my thumbs lightly into the depression of her hips.

"Shhhh. Listen. I don't know if I'm a good boxer because I notice all the details, or if I notice all the details because I'm a good boxer," I slowly licked up her inner thigh, working my way closer to her hips.

"But," I paused and looked up into her eyes.

"I *do* notice all the details. Like the day we met in your office. The yogurt cup in the trash. The plastic spoon. The *Running* magazine you had on your desk. I notice everything."

I continued to lick my way up her thighs. Half way between her knee and her pussy, I stopped and looked into her eyes again, "We encounter countless people in our lives, Kace. It's our responsibility to pay attention to who they are and notice how they affect us if we give them the chance. If we don't pay attention to life's details, we may miss these opportunities."

"I know who you are. I know what you do to me. Just having you near me fixes everything that is broken inside of me. All of my fucked up little pieces become one. I become whole when I'm near you. Understand that, Kace. I want you in my life. But one thing I will not do is *sacrifice* you for the sake of making me happy. You are vulnerable. I will not take advantage of that. Sex, to me, is sacred. If I have sex with someone, I am making the commitment to them and with them that I am willing to have a child with them. To me, it isn't as simple as sex. It's a commitment; a big one. If," I paused and smiled as I thought.

"Yes *if* the time comes, *and I hope it does*, I am going to fuck you until you are incapable of simple basic tasks. I'll even have to remind you how to breathe. For now, Kace," I ran my tongue along her inner thigh until I was an inch from her pussy.

"Ohhhh God," she whispered.

"Shhhhh, be quiet. Or you'll just get excited and blubber foolishness. Tap me once for yes and twice for no," I reminded her.

"For now, Kace. You'll wait. You'll wait until *I* am convinced whatever we decide to do is in *your* best interest. But believe me, I want you as bad as you want me. And when we make that commitment - if we do - you better be ready."

I buried my mouth on her pussy.

As I began to lick her pussy, she started moaning and pressed her hands into my shoulders. I pulled my right hand from her dress, and placed my cupped hand over her mouth. I slid my left hand under her butt cheek and raised her slightly off of the couch. With my tongue now deep inside her pussy, I worked my way to her clit. As my tongue made contact with her it, her body shuddered. I pressed my free hand firm against her mouth to silence her.

She tapped my shoulder once.

I pushed my mouth against her pussy and my tongue along her clit. I lowered my upper lip, pressing her clit between my lip and tongue. Using the tip of my tongue, I flicked her clit repeatedly and lightly until she began to thrust her hips. As her hips rose high, she screamed into my hand.

"Mmmmmmmm," her mouth opened and her teeth pressed against

the palm of my hand.

She released my shoulder with her right hand and tapped my back once. I continued to torture her clit with my tongue. She moved her hand back into place and squeezed my shoulders. Instinctively, she pulled her hips down into the couch cushion and started to wiggle away from me, pushing my shoulders away from her as she did. I lifted my hand from her face and wiped my mouth.

"Oh my fucking God, Shane," she said as she scooted across the couch cushions.

Quickly, she made as much distance as she could between us. She sat in the corner of the couch and stared at me as if she had no idea who I was.

Puzzled, I looked at her for a moment. The most beautiful woman in the world looked back at me as if she were in shock.

"Fucking kiss me," I said.

Immediately, she pounced across the couch and wrapped her arms around me. My hands on either side of her face, we kissed. Her full lips against mine, our tongues slowly searched for satisfaction. With my eyes closed, my mind found pure ecstasy in kissing Kace. Our lips slowly parted. As they did, I bit her lower lip, holding it firmly. She lightly moaned as I clenched it between my teeth. Without saying a word, I let go and slowly stood. As I reached for my shirt, she stared at my upper body.

"Who, Kace? Who's the most beautiful woman in the world?"

She pointed to her chest, "Me."

"Yes you are," I assured her.

Slowly, she shook her head and rolled her eyes.

"I could cum just watching you put on your shirt. You were right. I know it's been forever and a day, but you do *everything* perfectly, don't you?" she sighed as she grabbed her thong.

I smiled and pulled my shirt over my head.

"Fucker," she said as she pulled her panties over her feet.

As I reached for my hoodie, she slid her legs over the couch and attempted to stand.

"I can't feel my legs," she complained as she stood.

"I carried you in, I'll carry you out," I said as I zipped up my hoodie.

I reached down, picked her up, and hoisted her tight to my chest. As I carried her toward the door, she reached up and wrapped her arms around my neck. As I reached the door, she grinned, turned her head, and looked up into my eyes.

"Shane, I don't know how you'll know when the time has come. You know, when I'm *no longer vulnerable*. But when you decide *it's time* as you say," she paused and looked down at the floor.

"I like it rough. Think about that. And you better pray to God that *you're* ready," she said as she looked up.

Kace might only weigh one hundred pounds and barely be five feet tall, but when the time comes…

I'm going to have my hands full.

I know that.

SHANE

I have no complaints about my life. Life, as they say, is what we make it. I make mine a series of lessons. I learn something every day. And whatever I learn allows me to live the next day without the same worries, problems or concerns I have harbored in the past.

We are told to learn from our mistakes, and this will prevent us from repeating them. I live my life absorbing all of what is around me. I pay close attention to the mistakes people make and learn from them. It prevents me from having to make the same errors they have already made. We never know what the future may have in place for us, but remembering the events of the past allows us to walk into the future without much hesitation or wonder.

I feel as if I have lived the lives of many.

When you least expect it, life may propose something to you. Something you might not necessarily be looking for, but without a doubt it has the ability to offer your life some form of enrichment. When this time comes, all we can do is hope we are living in the particular day with an open mind, heart and arms.

Mike Ripton was one of life's proposals of enrichment.

"So. She said *Ripp, you have a stain on your shorts*. I looked down and was like, *what the fuck?* To tell you the truth I thought it was barbeque sauce," he paused and shrugged his shoulders.

"So she reaches down and tries to wipe it off. It was pretty cool she was willing to rub my leg, so I didn't grab her or anything. Anyway, she brushes my leg and says, *it looks like blood, and there's something in your pocket. And it's bleeding.* I freaked the fuck out," Ripp took a deep breath and raised his beer to his lips.

"So I start brushing my leg wondering what the fuck it is, and then it hits me. I got that fucking *finger* in my pocket. You carried Kace in the house, so I figured you two were fuckin'. I was like, *shit what to do?* So I turned around, reached into my pocket, and pulled out the finger. And when she wasn't lookin', I opened the grill and tossed that little nasty fucker inside. And it fell through the rack and into the fire. About five minutes, and she starts sayin' *something smells like burning flesh.* I acted like I couldn't smell it," he finished his beer and started rubbing his bald head with the palms of his hands.

I pulled my hood up and held it tight to my head. As I started to massage it into my cheeks, he picked up a fresh beer and continued.

"So that little motherfucker stunk up the whole yard. I'd already pulled half the chicken off the grill, but had the other half in there with that stinkin' ass three month old finger. It's smokin' and stinkin' and making me about half sick. The whole time, I'm acting like I can't smell nothin'. She's about to barf. I tell this bitch we were eatin' grapes earlier, and that was a crushed grape in my pocket. But here's the deal," he placed his beer on the table, leaned toward me, and opened his eyes wide.

"I put *that* chicken on the other side of the platter. The *finger chicken*. And that's the shit I gave to the girls," he held his eyes open

140

wide waiting for me to respond.

"God damn, Ripp. *The girls*? You fed that shit to Kace?" I asked as I pressed my hood into my face.

"Yep. Dude, I'm sorry, but it was just simple mathematics. Half the chicken was unharmed. That's a chicken and a half of the clean stuff. Luckily you weren't too hungry. Only reason I'm telling you is because you didn't actually eat any. Had you got into the dirty shit, I'd a kept my fuckin' mouth shut," he nodded his head and picked his beer back up off the table.

"I ain't shittin' ya. I'd a fed you that shit if I had to," he said as he tipped his beer bottle up.

"Fuck. You sick fucker. Let's keep this between us. *Forever*. I mean it, Ripp," I said as I opened the face of my hood with my hands.

"You bet," he said as he held out his clenched fist.

I clenched my fist and pounded it against his, confirming the conversation would never be discussed again.

"So now, after she ate the finger chicken, I ain't sure I can fuck with her. She's cute as fuck, but damn, dude. She ate the dirty shit," he raised one eyebrow and waited.

"*You* fed it to her," I paused for an instant, "*and you cut it off the guy*. You cut it off, and you *cooked* it, and you're worried about *her* being gross for eating chicken that was cooked with a finger you cut off and hid in the grill? Nasty assed chicken *you* fed her."

"See, that's why I keep you around. You always keep shit so real. Yeah, I never thought of it like that. I guess if they're giving prizes for bein' gross, cuttin' that fucker off and cookin' it trumps the finger chicken, huh?" he asked.

"I'd sure think so," I responded.

He nodded his head and took another drink of beer.

"Yeah. I might keep trying to fuck with her then. Guess you're gonna be fucking with Kace, and she ate a ton of that finger chicken. I can't really call or consider her gross, she's your girl and all," he smiled and nodded.

I shook my head and pulled off my hood.

"We're done with this, okay?" I asked.

"Alright, brother. Done," he said as he rubbed his hands together.

"Well, she seems nice. She's really pretty," I admitted.

"Yeah. She's hot. That's for sure," he laughed.

"I hate it when you call people hot. It's so fucking insensitive. All it really means is I want to fuck you. That's pretty much it," I complained.

"Yeah, but I *do* want to fuck her, bro'. Did you get a good look at her?" he raised his hands in wonder.

"I did. But seriously, Ripp. You want to fuck her based on the fact that she's tall, blonde, and has a nice ass," I sighed.

"Dude, I want to hurt that bitch. Well, you know. Hurt her in a good way. Shove her full of about ten inches of my pierced hard fuckin' cock. Fuck her 'till her legs are rubber and then watch her try and fuckin' walk," he smiled as he tipped his bottle of beer up.

I shook my head, "That's what brings parentless children into this earth. Broken marriages. Torn emotions."

I pulled the front of my hood up to my face.

"Dude, enough of the sorrow bullshit. Not everyone's as clean as you. Who dates a chic for three months after seeing her for a month *before* they started dating, and *doesn't* fuck her? I know of one person. *You*. You're a fucking weirdo. I've been telling you that for a few years now," he said as he pointed toward me.

"We're making progress. Don't fucking start. We've talked about this, Ripp. I don't want to hurt her. She's sensitive, vulnerable, and liable to make a decision based on something she *thinks* she needs, not what she actually *desires*. Like if your car breaks down, and someone gives you a car to drive. You drive whatever they give you. You drive it out of necessity, not desire. If you had the time to pick your own car, you'd damn sure pick something different. I want her to pick me because she feels she wants me, not because she needs to fill a hole in her soul with whatever she can stuff in there," I slipped my hands under my hoodie and felt my dog tags.

Ripp looked up at the ceiling for a moment. As he shifted his gaze to me, he took a shallow drink of his beer and swallowed it, "Yeah, but her car's been running like shit for about ten years, and broke down for what? Four? She ain't had sex in four years. She ain't making an uninformed decision. And if your car does happen to be broken down, and someone hands you a fucking Mercedes Benz, you don't drive that bad boy because you *have* to. You drive it because you know it's a damn fine ride. You're acting like you're some shitty assed dude, Dekk. You're not. We both know it," he pushed his empty beer bottle toward the center of the table.

"Well, we've been talking about going to see her mother. I've tried to talk her into letting me take her there. It's been about ten years since she's seen her. That's the first step for me. I want to do this right," I leaned onto the table and sighed.

Ripp rubbed the hair on his chin. He looked like he belonged on a surfboard in Los Angeles or on the beach at Venice. His head was always shaved, his body tan, and his chin had a patch of hair on it, always. No mustache, no typical male goatee, just a patch of hair on his chin. He rubbed it and stared at me, obviously thinking.

"You know. You watch guys play basketball. Sometimes you think you see a shot they ought to take, and you scream at the T.V, *take the shot*. Most of the time they don't, and you wonder why. Sometimes they do. But have you ever seen a guy take the time to shoot a basket and block his own shot?" he asked as his mouth began to form a smile.

I shook my head, "No, suppose not."

"Me neither. If they take the time to shoot, they're gonna let that fucker fly and see what happens. They took the risk when it left their fingertips. With Kace, dude, you're blocking your own shot. You took the time to seek her out after you met the first time at the video place. Did you forget that? You've been courting her for three months. *You shot*. Let that baby fly. Right into the basket," he rubbed his chin and smiled; confident he'd made his point.

I pulled the hood from my head and reached for my water glass. As I tipped it to my lips, I narrowed my gaze.

"Made sense, huh? The Ripper ain't no dummy, bro," he chuckled.

"Yeah, cooking that finger was a *smart* move," I responded dryly.

"Whoa. I thought we were done with that one?" he said as he pushed himself from the table and leaned into his chair.

"You're right. Sorry. And yeah, you made a good point. I'm thinking," I responded.

"Well, while you're thinking, think of this. There's two months till the fight. I'm thinking about taking off for a few months and helping you train. What do you think?" he asked as he leaned into the table.

"What do you mean, Ripp?" I asked as I leaned my chair forward.

"Simple. I'll spar with you. I'll watch the tapes of that dude, Mc Claskey. I'll mimic his style, and we'll spar as often as you want. I'll help push you physically. You know I'm a chameleon. I don't have a style. I'll become him. You can beat on me all you want. I want you to win this fucker for sure, Dekk. Hell, if you do. Shit. You'll be on the cover of Sports Illustrated," he tightened his jaw and made a fist.

I clenched my fist and extended my arm toward the center of the table.

"Do it,' he said.

I smacked my fist against his.

"Guess it's settled," he said.

"Guess so," I admitted.

"When you wanting to start?" he asked.

"Whenever you're ready," I responded, excited about training with Ripp.

"Let's start today. Just stay off this jaw," he said as he rubbed his jaw.

"You know I can't make any promises once I step into the ring, Ripp," I said apologetically.

"I know you can't. It's what makes you the beast you are. It's the devil inside of you. The one you're either fighting against or fighting for. Never seen another one like ya. You got that devil inside," he said as he stood and grabbed his wallet.

He was right.

And I needed to feed the demons.

KACE

There are instances in our lives we will never forget, no matter how hard we try. Other events, although we will attempt to retain those precious memories, somehow fade away. The recollection of yet other events will simply remain forever, stuck in the backs of our minds. We often remember the year, day, and sometimes even the hour associated with these special occurrences. Even the smell which lingered in the air will remain in our mind as a reminder of an event which we so preciously tucked away.

Ivan Pavlov, a Russian physiologist, in studying classical conditioning, had a theory about the human mind. He rang a bell each time he would feed his dog. Over time, the dog associated the ringing sound with an opportunity to obtain food. The scientist, in proof of this theory, would ring the bell, and watch the dog salivate at the sound of the bell alone.

"Babe, I'm home," Shane said as he walked in the front door.

"I'm in the kitchen," I replied as I moved the groceries around on the countertop.

As he walked into the kitchen, he unzipped his hoodie. He wasn't wearing a shirt underneath. He dropped his gym bag on the floor and walked behind me, wrapping his arms around my waist.

"Ripp and I just got done training. What are you making?"

He smelled clean, as if he had just taken a shower.

"I'm not really sure. Some kind of pasta. I bought wheat pasta, fresh basil, vegetables, and some lean beef. I was going to broil the meat and throw together a pasta dish. It sounded good. You want anything in particular?" I asked as I shuffled the groceries along the counter.

"I want *you*, Kace," he responded as he kissed the back of my neck.

A chill ran down my spine. Seeing Shane was enough to make me wet. Seeing Shane shirtless made me an uncomfortable mess. Having Shane touch me and talk to me sexually made me melt into a puddle on the floor.

His warm breath on my neck moved my thoughts from cooking to other things - scenes from the books I read. My books were both a blessing and a curse. Sometimes I felt as if I had actually experienced all of the things I read about. Truth be known, I have had minimal experience with sex but I was ready for that to change.

He raised his hands to my shoulders and turned me around to face him. Without speaking, he slid his hands from my shoulders to my neck. Softly, his hands moved up my neck to my face, cupping my cheeks in his hands as he kissed me. I closed my eyes and enjoyed the kiss as much as the first time we kissed. Kissing Shane was not kissing alone, it was *experiencing* - experiencing feelings and emotions which were unfamiliar to me. I felt *alive* when Shane kissed me. As my body tingled from head to toe, I smelled the sweet basil as I inhaled a breath through my nose.

"I could kiss you forever," he said as his face slowly moved away from mine.

I opened my eyes and focused on his face.

Bad idea.

It took every ounce of my ability to resist my desire to jump Shane's bones. I couldn't even look at him without thinking of sex. By simply coming home, he had given me a reason to feel alive, sexually.

But right now I was dying.

"Babe, what are you thinking?" he asked me, my face still in his hands.

You're a gorgeous, muscular, alpha male boxer. Really? More than anything I want you to fuck me unconscious.

He let go of my face and removed his unzipped hoodie, tossing it over the bar stool.

Oh, perfect. Add salt to the wound, Shane.

As he lowered his arms, his chest flared. The muscles on his stomach were rippled down to the 'V' that formed at his waist. His body defined physical perfection. As I admired his physique, I knew I must respond in some sane fashion.

"Babe?" he asked again.

"I just…" I paused, thinking of what to say next.

I inhaled and smelled the basil again. It was a calming fragrance. As I began to speak, he took a short breath. He seemed slightly nervous.

"Babe, it's time," he said as he reached down and began to remove his raggedy boots.

I froze.

"Time, time?" I muttered.

I felt flush and overly excited.

He nodded, "I want you to know something. This is not my opinion. It's not something I just say to say it. This is what I *feel*. Kace, I love you. It might seem strange to hear, it might not. But I know it just as sure as I know anything. I love you," he paused and looked down at his feet.

Officially melted.

"And," he looked up from the floor.

"The time has come," he tossed his boots into the living room and removed his socks.

Holy. Shit. Yes!

I closed my eyes and inhaled again, feeling as if it were a dream. I had no idea what to do, what to say, or where to move. I was stunned. I stood in the kitchen, clearly in some degree of shock, and stared. It had been four years. I wanted to tell him I loved him, but I couldn't speak; at least not intelligently. I wanted this to be perfect for him. I wanted it to be romantic. I wanted candles, rose petals and dimmed lights. I wanted slow passionate love making. I wanted to feel his body softly become one with mine. I heard his belt unbuckle. I opened my eyes.

Shane Dekkar naked.

His cock was thick, long, and twitched as it began to rise.

No love making.

No.

I wanted fucked.

Hard.

I yanked my top off and threw it somewhere. I began to fumble with my bra, but couldn't remember how to remove it. Slowly, he began to step toward me, reaching for my back.

"No!" I screamed.

What? I have no idea where that came from.

He stopped and looked at me, confused. I dropped my bra to the floor and unbuttoned my shorts. As I wrestled my shorts to the floor, he took another step toward me.

"No!" I screamed.

He stopped again, "Babe?"

I tried to think of every scene in every book I had read in the last four years on my Kindle. C.D. Reiss. E. L. James. Kylie Scott. Kendall Grey. My mind raced as I removed my panties. I began to get excited and feel like my thoughts were becoming jumbled.

Oh God. Not now. Let me speak.

"Like Ripp says," I blurted.

I could feel my pussy immediately get so wet it started to drip down my thighs. He looked at me as if I was crazy. I pointed at my mouth, rolled my eyes, and took a breath.

"I…"

"I got this," I muttered as I lowered myself to a squatting position.

"Babe, stand up," he said quietly as he held his hand out toward me.

I shook my head and held my hands out toward his muscled ass. I curled my index fingers toward my palms. I was done talking.

I got this.

He took a step toward me. I grabbed the backs of his thigh and pulled him closer. As his hips got close to my face, his cock stood straight up. I closed my eyes, opened my mouth, and took Shane Dekkar's perfect cock into my eagerly awaiting wet mouth.

He began to moan. He bent his knees and cupped my breasts in his hands.

He had probably waited as long for this moment as I, but there was no way he wanted it more than I did. I wanted him to remember this, and remember it good. Squeezing his rock hard ass in my hands, I slowly slid my mouth up and down his stiff cock. I moved my right hand from his ass to his balls. As I sucked and slurped along the shaft of his cock, I cupped his balls in my hand gently. He squeezed my breasts and closed his eyes. I pulled my mouth slowly from his cock and looked up at his face. A thin thread of saliva connected his cock to my lips.

I smiled and raised his cock from my lips with my hand. Softly, I began to suck his balls. He moaned and relaxed his leg muscles. I took his balls into my mouth, gently sucking and licking them like I had read about in the books. As I sucked his balls, he squeezed my breasts and pinched my nipples.

I licked along the shaft of his cock, and slowly slid my mouth down as far as I could. His cock was massive and thick, and I could only get about half of it into my mouth before my throat convulsed. I stroked his cock as I sucked it, moaning as I did.

As I attempted to take more of his cock into my mouth, I opened my eyes and looked up his muscular torso and at his face. His head was tilted back, and his eyes were still closed. I slurped and sucked as I slid my hands back and forth. His eyes opened for a moment, and he smiled as he looked down and squeezed my breasts. I reached down between my legs and touched my wet pussy. It was soaked and my clit was swollen. In a squatting position with my knees bent and my ass against my heels, I slowly spread my legs apart as I forced his cock into my throat. His focus changed from my face as he watched me slide a finger inside my wet pussy.

As soon as my hand brushed against my clit, I came. As I did, I closed my eyes and held his cock in my mouth. I felt his hands shift from my boobs to under my armpits. As he picked me up from the floor, I wrapped my arms around his shoulders. As I laid my head against his neck, I felt his warm breath on my ear.

"Kace, I know you're nervous. Just remember, tap me *once* for *yes*, and *twice* for *no*. That's all you need to be able to do, okay?" he whispered.

Excited, I tapped his back once with my hand.

He carried me to the kitchen counter and lifted me to on top, placing my ass on the countertop. His hands slid down my torso to my inner thighs and gently spread my legs apart. As he lowered his head between my legs, he pushed against my chest softly, forcing me to go from sitting to lying down.

His mouth softly pressed against my pussy and his finger slid inside. As he began to lick my pussy, his finger gently worked in and out in a rhythmically predictable motion. I closed my eyes and focused on the feeling. Within a few seconds, I felt as if I was going to explode.

I tapped him once.

He continued the same rhythm and motions. I arched my back and began to moan.

"Ohhhhhhh…"

"Ohhh…"

"Oh."

"Oh."

I raised my butt from of the countertop and came hard as my leg muscles tensed. I had never felt anything like it in my life, nor did I have any idea these types of feelings even existed. I opened my eyes and looked around the kitchen, making sure I wasn't dreaming. For a moment, my mind was elsewhere, lost in a sea of emotional bliss.

His tongue slid to my clit, and began to press it between his lip and the tip of his tongue. Sparks shot through my lower body and up my spine. Scared, I raised my head from the countertop, looked him in the eyes, and tapped his shoulder twice.

"Crazy," I blurted.

He raised his hand to his mouth.

"Electricity," I muttered.

I'm just going to keep my mouth shut. This is ridiculous.

He held his index finger to his lips, "Shhhhh."

He returned to the same fingering and licking motions which had earlier brought me to climax. I kept my eyes open and watched as he licked and fingered me. The sight of his muscular back and shoulders was more than I was prepared for. As his tongue worked me into a frenzy, his finger began to bring me to climax. I closed my eyes and bit my lower lip.

My breathing became labored.

I bit my lip harder.

I felt my emotions begin to peak. It was as if I was going to explode from every pore in my body. I started to shake. His motions predictable and pleasurable, I anticipated the climax. As it came, I bit my lip harder.

This is going to hurt.

"Ahhhhhh…"

"Fuck. Fuck. Fuuuuck…"

I sounded like a retarded sailor. I bucked my hips against his face and exploded.

"Holy!" I screamed as I climaxed.

And I came. Hard.

My body shuddered.

And I came again.

His finger worked in and out of my pussy. I raised my hips.

And I came again.

I trembled. I was done. That was it. I wanted to die, right here there the kitchen, beside my precious basil.

Ahhh, the smell of the sweet basil.

My mind went blank. As I opened my eyes, the room was dark. I could still feel his mouth on my pussy and his tongue inside of me, but I could not see. I blinked my eyes.

Blurry.

I blinked again.

A silhouette.

Again.

Shane Dekkar.

Holy fuck. I am in no way prepared for anything like this. I'm just not.

I thought of the scenes in my books. They lasted much longer. The sex goes on and on and on. Sometimes they have sex in several different positions. *God, I'm going to have to find some form of energy and try and control these earth shattering orgasms.* Maybe if I didn't look at him, it will be easier.

I'll keep my eyes closed.

That should do it.

I closed my eyes.

I felt nothing. He wasn't touching me. I wondered if we were done.

I opened my eyes.

JesusfuckingChrist.

He stood in front of the counter, stroking his cock in his right hand.

I slapped the counter once.

Startled, he jumped and wrinkled his brow. His stroke slowed down.

No no no. I love it. Stroke it for me please. I'm in fucking heaven.

Still lying on my back, I raised my fists above the countertop about six inches and gave him the thumbs up sign. I nodded my head sharply.

His pace sped up slightly.

I tapped the counter once.

Both thumbs up.

He stepped to the side of the counter, steadily stroking his cock. As he approached the edge, he grabbed my calves and pulled me to the side of the countertop. With my ass half hanging over the edge, He slowly pressed the tip of his cock into my soaking wet pussy.

Ohgoodfuckinggod.

This will never work.

I leaned up and slapped his thigh twice.

A million little thoughts ran through my head. I wondered if it was possible that his cock wouldn't fit inside my pussy. I had never considered it, but I guessed I never really asked anyone if they had heard of it happening before. As he began to pull out, I slapped his leg once, focused, and let out one word.

"Slow," I sighed.

He nodded his head and looked down at my pussy as he guided himself inside me again. As I felt him pressing inside of me, I took a deep breath and relaxed. The feeling of his huge cock pressing inside of me prevented me from relaxing much, and I became frustrated.

I bit my bottom lip as his cock slowly pushed deep into my wet pussy. It felt like it was in my chest. I exhaled, and took a slow breath. He held his cock deep inside of me, leaned forward, and began to squeeze my breasts.

"Kace," he said softly.

I looked up.

"Relax, babe. Breathe," he said.

I nodded. As I felt his cock begin to slide out, I pressed my elbows onto the counter and raised my shoulders. I looked down and watched in amazement as his cock slid in and out of my wet pussy. As I watched him fuck me, I felt as if seeing it happen made it much easier. If it was even possible, it felt as if seeing it made me more lubricated and wet. I watched eagerly as his glistening cock slid in and out of my soaking wet pussy. Each stroke became easier, and I got lost in watching him fuck me.

His stomach muscles flexed as he stood on his tip-toes and slowly pushed himself in and out of me. I focused on his body and watched him admiring mine as his hands now held my upper thighs.

I began to feel as if pressure was building up inside of me. I pressed down on my bottom lip with my teeth. The feeling of having Shane fuck me was almost too much for me to take. I began to tingle and I felt my breathing change. I was sure I was preparing to have an orgasm, and without a doubt it was going to kill me.

Remembering what I had told him at Ripp's house a few weeks prior, I wondered what he must be thinking.

But when you decide it's time, as you say - know this. I like it rough. Think about that. And you better pray to God that you're ready...

I stopped biting my lip and looked Shane in the eyes. As he looked at me and smiled, his perfect white teeth gleamed. Again, I thought of everything I had read on my Kindle over the past few years. I opened my mouth and stared at Shane's face.

"Shhhh," he said softly as he forced himself in and out of me.

I shook my head from side to side.

"Fuck," I inhaled slowly after the word came out.

"Fuck me," I exhaled as I spoke.

I can do this.

"Fuck me hard, Shane. Fuck me hard. Please," I begged.

He sped up his pace.

I shook my head and waved my arms in the air like a child wanting to be picked up by his mother.

He moved his hands from my waist to my armpits, and lifted me up. He slid his forearms under my armpits, his hands behind my back, and lifted me from the counter. I wrapped my arms around his neck, my legs around his waist, and laid my head on his shoulder. Immediately, I felt calm.

I whispered in his ear, "No. Fuck me. Please. Fuck me. I want to remember this."

He began thrusting his hips upward, his upper thighs and hips bouncing against my ass as his cock slid deep inside of me.

"Against the wall," I begged.

I'd seen the pictures on Tumblr at work of women being fucked against the wall by a muscular man. I wanted it. As he carried me to the wall I became more excited. As I felt my back against the cold surface, I tensed and took a quick breath.

"Do it," I growled.

He slid his hands from my back to under my ass. Slowly, he began to fuck me against the wall, his hands cupped under my ass cheeks. I closed my eyes, thinking of the books, the pictures and the fact we had finally made it to this point.

"Harder," I pleaded as I bit his neck.

He tilted his head toward me, trying to force my mouth off of his neck. I bit harder and grunted through my clenched teeth.

"Hrrrder" I grunted.

He began to forcefully fuck me, shoving his entire cock into me. Each thrust lifted my body six inches. As soon as my body slid back down, he would thrust against me again.

Yes, this is what I want.

"Hrrrder" I begged through my clenched teeth, biting his neck harder.

"Fuck Kace," he grumbled, twisting his neck against my bite.

I released my grip on his neck.

"He speaks," I breathed into his ear.

"Well, you weren't saying shit," he said as he pressed me to the wall.

"I was nervous," I gasped as he softly pressed me into the wall.

"I'm fine now," I grunted as he started thrusting harder into me.

"You aren't going to hurt me," I whispered into his ear.

"Now fuck me like I want," I bit his neck again.

He began forcefully fucking me into the wall. With each stroke he increased his force and speed. My head began to hit the wall. I slapped his back once and bit his neck harder.

"Hrrrder" I begged though my teeth.

He pounded me into the wall.

I felt my pussy contracting as his massive cock thrust in and out of my now soaked pussy. His cock felt as if it were growing. He kept fucking me into the wall with each stroke. I closed my eyes and bit his neck.

This.

This is what I want.

My breathing became short and shallow. It was as if I almost forgot to breathe. His cock swelled. I released my grip on his neck and moved my mouth to his ear.

Yes, I want this.

"Cum inside of me. Fill me with cum, Shane. I want to feel it," I whispered into his ear.

His breathing became choppy and he closed his eyes. I felt myself begin to climax in a manner I had no I was capable of. As if my body was warning me, I tensed up and focused as I squeezed his body against me.

"Kace," he said.

"Kaaaace," he repeated slowly and softly.

"Do it," I sighed.

I closed my eyes.

"Oh fuck. Oh fuck…Ooooh fuuuuck," I heard the words somehow escape my mouth.

I felt his cock swell and ejaculate as he groaned. At the same time, whatever was trapped inside of me released - as if I had actually exploded. I gasped for a breath. I felt cum running down my legs. I could not speak or think. Caught in the particular moment, I simply blinked my eyes. Finally, my eyes began to focus. When I looked at his face, I saw relief. Not an orgasm worth, but a lifetime.

I leaned back into the wall, still incapable of speech. I took a slow breath and exhaled.

Ahhh. Basil.

I reached up and pushed his head back. As I looked into his steel grey eyes, I leaned forward and softly kissed the most beautiful man in the world.

And finally, I was able to speak.

"I love you, too," I said softly.

And I began to cry.

SHANE

In my experiences with life I had often searched for something or someone to satisfy a void. When I did, I often settle for something substandard or second rate. I did so because I felt I must fill an opening. When I did not look or attempt to resolve a particular deficiency, I often stumbled onto what it is that I actually needed. Life tends to provide us with our most valuable assets when we least expect it or while we're not even particularly looking.

In life, we need to pay the closest attention when we aren't paying attention at all.

Life has a way of sneaking up on us.

This, in itself, was why I paid attention to all of the little details.

Because I didn't like surprises.

"So, you think you're going to be alright, babe?" I asked as we turned the corner into the residential neighborhood.

"I think so, as long as you're close by. You make me feel really comfortable. I don't get excited anymore around you," she giggled.

"Nervous?" I asked.

"Duh," she sighed.

"How long?" I asked.

"I don't know for sure, I think it's been ten years. I'm not really sure.

I don't remember. It's been a long time. Since before I graduated high school if I remember right," she said.

No different than I, Kace didn't remember a tremendous amount of her childhood. Her memories - or lack of memories - lasted into her teens. I suppose her problems lasted longer as well. I didn't remember my childhood because I was moved around and my father was gone. She didn't remember because she had events or circumstances her mind chose to set aside.

Coming from the background she came from, it was no surprise to see her mind set aside memories associated with abuse. One funny thing about the human mind was that it would often set aside a period of time – maybe even a few years – to get rid of a few memories or particular events.

Kace hadn't initially told me, but eventually she admitted her father had abused her mother physically. Her mother finally left her father after many years of being beaten. Kace, at the time, was about twelve years old. Being exposed to this type of abuse generally made the children either totally opposed to abuse or an abuser themselves. It seemed to depend on the person and how their mind processed it.

"By the GPS, we're just a few blocks, you sure you're alright?" I asked.

"My stomach feels funny. But you can't fix it. Just go, I'll be fine," she responded.

I was glad we decided to come see her mother at this point in time, long before the holidays. It might allow Kace to make the adjustments needed, possibly allowing her to see her family during the Thanksgiving and Christmas holidays.

"Well, here we are, house number 648," I said as we pulled up to the front of the home.

She swallowed heavily.

"You alright?" I asked.

"Yeah," she sounded like she had a frog in her throat.

"Babe, any time you're ready to go just tell me so. I'm damn near as nervous as you," I chuckled lightly.

She nodded.

"Who, babe? Who's the most beautiful woman in the world?" I asked.

She pointed to her chest and smiled, "I am."

"Yes, babe. You are," I said as I leaned toward her seat and kissed her.

"Ready?" I asked.

She opened the door to the truck and got out.

I guess that means yes.

Kace was one of the strongest women I had ever met. She was a true survivor. One hundred pounds of *tough.* As I fumbled with the door handle, she stepped around to my side of the truck and waited. Finally, I opened the door and stepped outside the truck.

"Alright, let's do this," I said as I held my arm out to my side.

After she attached herself to my arm, we walked up the sidewalk together to the front porch of the house. As I reached out to ring the buzzer, the door slowly opened.

"Oh dear Lord. The pictures didn't do you any justice. Kace, you're beautiful," a woman said through the opened door. She was petite, blonde, and very pretty.

"Come in," she said.

As she held her arms out, they began to shake. We stepped inside the home, and Kace immediately hugged her mother. Ten years of sorrow began to run down the cheeks of both women as they embraced. The sounds of sobbing muffled the sound of everything else.

"I'm sorry," Kace sobbed as she wrapped her arms around her mother's shoulders.

"No, baby. I'm so sorry. I never should have let you go," her mother apologized as she began to cry uncontrollably.

I stepped to the side of the doorway, feeling somewhat uncomfortable with the situation. Seeing Kace crying was not easy for me. Seeing people cry, in general, was difficult for me; especially women. Feeling somewhat helpless, I found a chair and sat quietly as they stood and cried in each other's arms. Slowly, I pulled my hood up over my head and pressed the soft fabric into the sides of my face. Eventually, they walked into the living room and sat down side-by-side on the couch. I watched them exchange short embarrassed glances at each other as they covered their mouths and tried to stop crying. Eye makeup streamed down each of their faces.

"I missed you so much," Kace sobbed.

"I missed you, Kace," her mother whimpered as she leaned over and kissed Kace's forehead.

Her mother stood, looked at me, back toward Kace, and sat down as if she were confused on what to do or how to digest the entire reunion. Overcome with emotion, her mind appeared to be having a difficult time deciding the proper thing to do with the situation. I realized not seeing or talking to your child in a decade; and then trying to start over as if nothing happened would be difficult at best.

"Oh God, this is too much, Kace. I feel like I'm going to have a heart attack," her mother said as she held her hand against her chest.

Her breathing was short and choppy as she tried to control her sobbing.

"Mother, don't say that," Kace smiled and wiped her eyes as she spoke.

Finally.

They're smiling.

Her mother laughed between sobs. As they hugged again, I relaxed and leaned back into the chair. Watching someone cry tears of joy can be uplifting. Watching someone cry tears of sorrow has always caused me to feel helpless. In my opinion, this was a combination of both. My emotions were riding a roller coaster and I felt I couldn't see the track ahead.

"So, this is Shannon?" her mother asked as she stood again.

"No mother. *Shane*," Kace responded.

As her mother approached, I stood. As she opened her arms and reached for me, I met her with a heartfelt hug. As we embraced, she sighed.

"I'm so glad you saved her," she said as she released me from her grasp.

Before I could respond, Kace spoke up.

"Mother, *I saved myself.* Shane has just been here for me. He talked me into seeing you. I've been scared. If anyone knows, *you know*," Kace took a breath and wiped her face.

"Oh look at us with our makeup all over our faces, come on," her mother said as she grabbed Kace's hand and led her away.

I felt even more at ease as I heard them laughing and talking in the bathroom. A mother and her daughter reunited after an extended length of time. I exhaled and relaxed. I thought of my father, and how long he had been gone. It had only been a few years since his death, but seeing him now would be gut wrenching at best. I recalled all of the time he was away when I was young, and seeing him when he would return from war. The initial excitement of seeing him was almost overwhelming. Sometimes, I felt as if I was going to vomit. After some time, my emotions settled, and I felt as if he had never left. When it was time for his next deployment, I would become angry and short tempered. My father's company, although sacred, was a difficult time for me emotionally.

They walked back into the room laughing. As if I knew what each of them felt, I sensed I could predict what emotions they would feel throughout the meeting, based on my many similar meetings with my father. As my body relaxed, I slumped into the soft chair, and got lost in the memories of my father, my childhood, and my love for both. Almost immediately, I began to feel as if I were going to fall asleep.

Pulling the blankets tightly over his head, the sounds of the screaming were muffled. The closed bedroom door and the television on the other side of the wall prevented the little boy from hearing details.

As much as he feared what he may hear, he yeared to know. Slowly, he pulled the blankets away from his face, in an attempt to hear what was on the other side of the wall. His face barely visible and his head still covered, he peered through the opening he had created in the blankets.

From the other side of the wall, a muffled scream could be heard.

The little boy covered his head.

A dull thud.

The little boy uncovered his face, rubbing the soft fabric of the blanket into the sides of his cheeks.

Two voices, almost inaudible, alternated screams.

Another dull thud.

The little boy covered his face with the blanket, buried his head into the pillow, and cried.

As he lay in the only safe place he knew, the boy found comfort in the shelter of the blanket which lay atop his bed. It was there that he could always find comfort and peace.

Serenity.

There, with his face covered, he was always safe.

KACE

What we try to remember and what we prefer to forget. Our mind doesn't always have an understanding of how we want to sort things. Sometimes a simple memory can be enough to defeat even the toughest of souls.

Acceptance of these memories as being in the past, and understanding they are nothing more than a reminder can often allow us to continue through life without feeling guilt, sorrow, or shame. Not accepting them as such can allow us to be overcome by the emotion associated with the memory.

"Shane. Baby, you fell asleep," I said as I tugged on his arm.

He pulled his arm away from me and pressed his hood against his face.

"Baby?" I said softly as leaned over him.

He pulled against the sides of his hood and looked out of the opening.

"Oh," he paused and looked around the room.

"Sorry," he said as he sat up in the chair.

"I must have fallen asleep," he apologized as he pulled his hood from his face.

His face was covered in sweat.

"It's hot in here, baby. You shouldn't wear your hoodie," I said as I leaned into the chair to kiss him.

"Where's your mother?" he asked as he looked around the room.

I steadied his face with my hands and looked into his eyes, "She's making lunch for us," I said as I pressed my lips against his.

As if the kiss woke him up totally, he held me in his arms and kissed me deeply. "Kace, you mean the world to me," he said.

"You mean the world to me," I responded.

"No, I mean. Well, fuck. I don't know what I'm trying to say. I just. I don't know. I want to spend the rest of my life being everything you want in a man. I want to make up for what you haven't received in life. I want to always be here for you. I want so much for you to be happy," he said.

"What got into you? I *am* happy," I responded.

"An entirely different degree of happy," he said as he stood up and pulled his hoodie off.

I smiled, "Okay, sounds good."

He looked around the room as he tossed his hoodie on the back of the chair. He rubbed his eyes and turned to focus on my face. Slowly, he smiled.

"How long was I out?" he asked.

"I don't know. We talked a while. I heard you snore after a bit. We just decided to leave you be. I thought you were worn out from all of the training for the fight. Is that okay?" I asked.

"No, babe. It's fine," he said as he stretched his arms behind his back.

"While she's cooking, you wanna look at some stuff with me?" I asked excitedly.

"Sure, what do ya got?" he asked as he rubbed his hands together.

"Well, mom said she had all my stuff from when I was in high school in a spare room. She saved everything. I want to go look at it. I might want to take a few things home," I giggled as I rubbed my hands together jokingly.

As we both stood and rubbed our hands together, I got excited. I was eager to see things I hadn't seen in ten years. Things I had long since forgotten. The old memories were going to be nice to sift and sort through. Not knowing what I may encounter was exciting. I tried to recall what she might have set aside, and the excitement almost overcame me.

"Well?" I asked.

"Let's go," he said.

"Mom, we're going to go snoop," I screamed into the kitchen.

"Okay, have fun. There's a foot locker beside the bed," my mother's shallow voice responded.

I opened the door and Shane and I stepped inside. Immediately, I felt a wave of heat come over me. I began to shake lightly.

My Hello Kitty comforter was on the bed. I snuggled under that comforter for forever. Josh and I first...

Fucking Josh.

I turned and looked at the wall. All of my medals from running in track were on the wall in a shadow box. My throat felt full, and a lump rose in my throat as I walked toward the box. Newspaper clippings were framed on each side of the display. I walked to the framed pages and looked at the dates.

"Oh my God. This was my senior year - after I left. She kept them, Shane. She kept them," I said as I pointed at the framed articles.

Several of the awards were for first place running in long distance. I always liked running, it allowed me to clear my head. The habit of running had stuck with me and become one of the few things I looked forward to. A five mile run could clear my mind like nothing else. I turned and looked at Shane.

"Fun, huh?" he said as he looked around the room at my things.

It was truly a step back in time and almost overwhelming. I gazed at the foot of the bed and wondered what was in the locker on the floor. I knelt down beside it and placed my hands on top of the locker. I looked up at Shane.

"Come here, babe. Let's see what's in here," I said as I pointing to the locker.

I placed both of my hands on the top of the lid.

Shane knelt down beside me and sat cross legged on the floor. He turned, put his arm around my shoulder, and pulled me close to him. As I leaned into him, he kissed me softly on the lips. I pressed my thumbs under the top of the trunk lid as he kissed me.

"Babe, I'm so glad we're here," he said as our lips parted.

"So am I," I responded as I took a deep breath.

He turned and looked at the locker as I opened the lid. A musty smell came out as it opened. My dresses, my shirts, my pants, my skirts - all folded nicely. I turned and looked at Shane, excited to see all of the things I hadn't seen in ten or more years. A rush of emotion filled me.

"Babe, look," I said as I sorted through the articles of clothing.

I picked up a dress from my sophomore year in school and smelled it. Holding it in my arms, I turned toward Shane. He gazed into the foot locker and rubbed his dog tags frantically with his right hand.

Something's wrong.

His lip was quivering.

"Babe," I said softly.

As he started to stand, he reached under his shirt and grabbed ahold of his dog tags.

"Babe," I said as I stood up.

Something's bad wrong.

I heard a *snap.*

His hand came out from under his shirt, holding the broken chain in his hand. He turned and looked at me as if he were in a trance.

And as the dog tags fell from his hand, Shane Dekkar collapsed into a motionless pile on the floor.

KACE

Having what we hold dear to our heart pulled from our grasp puts things - all things - in perspective. Not knowing when or if the object we love will be returned allows us to truly understand just exactly how deeply that object was embedded in our life.

"I need to know what's going on," I begged.

"I'm sorry ma'am. You'll just have to wait until someone can see you," the nurse responded.

"Is there someone else I can talk to?" I asked frantically.

"No. There is no one else. I'll have a doctor come see you as soon as someone knows something," she said over the top of the nurse's station.

I put my hands on my hips, looked down at the floor and wanted to cry. I refused to become weak. I needed to be strong for Shane. I looked up and down the hallway as I heard someone running my direction.

Thank God.

Ripp.

I held my arms out in front of me and flapped my hands.

As he picked me up from the floor and into his arms, I felt comfortable. I was no longer alone. I felt so helpless and incapable up until Ripp arrived. After a moment of holding me, he lowered me back down onto the floor.

"I got here as soon as I got your voicemail. You didn't answer your phone," he gasped.

My eyes began to well with tears.

"What happened?" he asked.

"I don't know," I began to cry.

I wiped my eyes and took a breath, "He just. He. We were in my mother's new house. He just woke up from a nap. We started looking at stuff in a footlocker full of my old junk. He seemed really weird. But he stood up and pulled his dog tags off. It was like he wanted them off. And then he just collapsed. When the ambulance got there, he was…" I started crying and couldn't continue.

"It's okay Shorty. I'm here until they release him. So, what happened when the ambulance came?" Ripp asked as he hugged me lightly.

I thought about what Shane was doing and I began to tremble, "He was just in a ball on the floor. Like he was…"

"Uhhm, like his brain didn't work anymore. He didn't blink or talk or anything," I sobbed.

"Oh. Fuck. What are they saying now?" he asked as he released me and wiped the tears from my face.

"Nothing. She won't tell me anything," I said as I pointed to the nurse's station.

"Stand over there," he said as he motioned to the other side of the hallway.

Confused, I stepped to the other side of the hallway. As I leaned on the wall I studied Ripp. Dressed in his cargo shorts, sneakers and a tank top, he was rather intimidating to those who didn't know him. He turned to the nurse's station, gripped the edge of the desk top in his hands, and took a deep breath. As he started talking, his voice was very matter-of-fact and direct.

"I'm Mike Dekkar, Shane's brother. I need to know what his status is. He was brought in by ambulance," he said to the nurse as he leaned onto the top tier of the station.

The nurse took a breath, sighed, and looked up at Ripp.

"Sir, I told his wife a moment ago *I don't know*. If you'd like to go wait in the waiting room, I'll have an answer for you in a little while. I'll have someone come see you in a bit," as she finished speaking she looked down at her keyboard.

Ripp sharply knocked on the countertop with is knuckles three times to get the nurses attention. Annoyed, she looked up. Ripp immediately started again.

"Listen, I don't have *a little while*. I have about this much fuckin' patience, lady," he held his hand in the air and snapped his fingers loudly.

"Look at me," he demanded as he stepped away from the raised counter.

He pointed at himself from head to toe. His arm, neck, and leg muscles rippled as he pointed his finger up and down his muscular body.

"Do I look like a guy you want to piss off?" he stepped toward the counter, leaned against it, and flexed his chest muscles.

"This mother fucker is *full* of doctors. *Find one*. Go find one and get him to go find my brother. And then find out what the fuckin' deal is or I'm going to start knocking mother fuckers out..." he whispered loudly.

He turned his head from side-to-side and surveyed the hallway. After realizing the entire corridor was empty, he turned toward the nurse and finished his sentence.

"Cold."

She looked up into Ripp's eyes.

"Sir, I'll call security," she said as she put her hand on the phone at the lower desk.

"Call 'em. Fuck yes," he said as he rubbed his hands together.

"Call 'em. I'll knock them the fuck out too. It's what I do. I knock motherfuckers out. Cold. Call security, and while you're at it call the fuckin' cops. Tell 'em to send the S.W.A.T. team. They'll need all the help they can get, because I hate fucking cops," he was starting to become a little louder and was having a difficult time whispering.

"Your best bet is this, lady. Find a doctor and find out what the fuckin' deal is. In the next ten God damned minutes. We'll be in the waiting room, waitin'," he pushed himself from the countertop and stared.

"C'mon, Shorty," he said as he held out his right hand.

I leaned away from the wall and stepped toward him.

"Why'd you make me stand over there?" I asked as I reached for his hand.

"I didn't want you to get any debris on you if I started breaking shit," he said as we walked down the hallway toward the waiting room.

"Ripp?" his hand in mine, I looked up toward his face.

"Yeah, Shorty," he responded as he angrily stomped his way toward the waiting room.

I needed comfort, reassurance and some form of confirmation everything was going to be alright – including me. I felt all jumbled up inside. The man I loved dearly was in the trauma unit in the hospital and I didn't know what was wrong or how to fix it.

"I love you," I said, still holding his hand in mine.

He stopped walking and turned to face me.

"Shorty, I love you too. You're my brother's girl. Any time he's gone, I gotta take care of ya. It's just how we do it here in Texas," he smiled.

And he immediately started walking again.

How we do it here in Texas.

Knocking motherfuckers out.

Cold.

SHANE

"I don't think that had anything to do with it, Ripp," I said as I sat up in the hospital bed.

"Well, why they want to keep ya over night? Don't make sense," Ripp responded.

"I don't think Shane would be nervous about the fight either. He fights all the time, and never gets nervous. It's probably a lot of things. Diet, training, nerves, everything combined," Kace said from the edge of the bed as she squeezed my hand.

"Well, they can say you had a nervous meltdown, but if they want to keep ya for more tests, they don't *know* shit. I'm gonna talk to that prick when he comes in here," Ripp said.

"Ripp, leave it alone. Just let them do their tests, and I'll be out of here in the afternoon tomorrow. It's not a huge deal. I guarantee you it's nothing else. He's signing a release for me to fight," I assured him.

"Well, that's the biggest thing. I don't want you lying to me, you fucker. Having a fucking brain hemorrhage or something and telling me it's a hemorrhoid," he laughed.

"Not gonna happen, bro," I said.

Kace turned my direction, squeezed my hand, and smiled. I couldn't ask for a better woman than her. Finding someone who was more

181

devoted to me, supportive of my career and generally concerned for my well-being would be impossible. Kace was a beautiful woman in her appearance as well as in her being. I squeezed her hand and smiled in return.

"Well, what about training?" Ripp asked as he paced back and forth across the floor.

"Ripp it's fine. Jesus, go home. I'll be back in training in the next day or so. There's nothing to worry about. Just go home and get some sleep. You two need to go eat anyway. And I'm beat, I need to get some sleep," I said in an effort to convince him to leave and relax.

"Yeah, I imagine you are tired, with all those tests they ran on ya. Fuckin' idiots. I'm hungrier than a motherfucker. What time is it?" Ripp asked.

"Ten after eight," Kace responded.

"Yeah, maybe we ought to let the man sleep. How you gonna get out of here tomorrow?" Ripp asked.

"Well, one of you two can come get me. She has to work in the morning, so I imagine it'll be you," I said as I smiled at Kace.

She scowled at me and squeezed my hand in an exaggerated fashion.

"Oh, shit that hurts," I joked as I pulled my hand away from her grasp.

"You're gonna think *hurt*. I'm going to come when he gets you," Kace said as she slapped my shoulder.

"We'll both come and get him, Shorty. I'll come get you, and we'll both come up here. How's that?" Ripp asked.

"Sounds good," Kace responded.

"Well, if you're sure you'll be alright, we'll get out of here," Ripp said.

"Yeah. I'll be fine, and we'll all go out tomorrow and eat or something, I just need to sleep," I said as I held my hand to my mouth to cover a fake yawn.

Kace stood from the edge of the bed and leaned over to kiss me, "I'm sorry, all of this just scared me. I'll see you tomorrow, Shane."

"Don't worry. I'll be fine," I responded.

"Love ya, bro," Ripp said as he held his fist over the bed.

I clenched my hand into a fist and pounded it against Ripp's hand. He pounded against mine in return.

"Alright, let's do this," Ripp said as he put his arm around Kace.

"Take care of her, Ripp," I said as they faced the door.

Ripp turned his head, looked over his shoulder and said what I expected him to.

"I got this," he smiled.

I got this.

Ripp was better at being a friend than most people were at being family. We are stuck with our family; we don't get to choose them. We choose our friends, and I was certainly glad I chose Ripp. As I lay in bed, I wish I could have chosen my family. I reached up to my neck to make sure my dog tags were gone.

I never wanted to see them again.

The doctor ran every type of test he could to determine if there was brain damage. After all of the tests results came in with the same result - *negative,* I told the truth about what I knew regarding my collapse. I didn't know what caused it, but I knew to some degree what I felt immediately before it had happened. Additionally, I could clearly see the differences in myself afterward.

Some strange combination of Kace seeing her mother, the crying, and emotion triggered a nightmare while I was asleep in the living room. When Kace and I walked into the bedroom, I felt strange. When she opened the footlocker, something inside of me snapped. My head filled with the memories of my childhood, depicted as a dozen little movies all trying to play inside my head at once.

It was more than I could make sense of, but any fool would have been able to understand the content of the memories. They were all the same.

My father was beating my mother.

I'm not certain if I chose at some point in time in my life to rid myself of those memories, or if my brain naturally did it to try and let me live in some form of peace. I know for my entire adult life I have not been able to recollect any memories of my childhood. I had always attributed the lack of memory to the fact we shuffled around from house to house when I was a child.

I now knew the memory loss had nothing to do with moving from home to home. Now, as I lay in the hospital bed, I was beginning to recall memories of my entire childhood.

And I didn't like any of it.

My father was a savage.

My mother left when I was a child. Now, I knew why. I had spent my late teens and entire adult life standing up for every woman who had been abused and now I had a clear understanding why I felt such a desire to assist them. I wanted to vomit. As I tried to make sense of what was developing in my head, the door opened the door.

"Dekkar? Shane Dekkar?" the doctor asked.

I sat up in bed, "Yes sir."

"How are you feeling?" he asked as he approached the bed.

"Fine sir. I'm a little confused. I have new memories running around in my head and it's strange, really strange. Hard to explain," I said as I rubbed my temples with both hands.

"The human mind is a fabulously complex piece of equipment," he stated as he leaned closer to me and looked into my eyes with a light.

"Well, I have a thousand questions," I said as I tossed my legs over the bed.

"I'm afraid I probably won't have any of the answers you're looking for. I'm a family practice doctor. You're going to need to talk to a psychiatrist. We're going to want to keep you here until tomorrow, if that's alright with you. I think it will be best," he said as he leaned away from the bed.

"Well, I have some questions about not so much why this happened, but what to do now?" I asked.

"Again, I'm not going to be a big help. Actually, I really won't be any help at all. There are considerable improvements a psychiatrist can make, I'm sure. He can address everything tomorrow. Get some sleep and we'll talk in the morning," he said as he approached the foot of the bed.

"Improvements? I don't want improvements. I need this to stop," I pleaded.

"Again, I can't do anything for you right now. I can get you something to help you sleep, but that's about it," he responded in a matter-of-fact tone.

I shook my head. Drugs were the last thing I wanted, "No, I'll be fine. Tomorrow it is."

He nodded his head and walked out.

I raised my legs up onto the bed and relaxed. As I looked at the ceiling, it wasn't what I necessarily wanted to admit, but any recovery from the memories was going to be on my own. There wasn't a doctor, psychiatrist or psychologist who was going to cure me.

Without a doubt, they would all tell me the same thing.

You'll need to just accept it. The sooner you do, the sooner you'll start healing.

I closed my eyes and attempted to come to terms with the fact my father was a man I would beat the absolute hell out of if I was given a chance.

SHANE

"Yes, as a matter of fact, he was a Marine," I answered in response to the doctor's question regarding my father's military background.

"Well, the human mind is difficult to understand. We all deal with stress, memories, and the repression of memories differently. Our mind often, as a survival skill of sorts, places memories on a back shelf. Over time, we forget they even exist. In our conscious mind they *aren't* a memory. Like a deleted movie scene, if that makes sense," the doctor paused and tapped his pen on the desk.

"Look at it this way. You have a favorite movie. It resembles many other movies by the same director with the same cast. You watch it one time, just once. You recall a fondness for the movie a few years later, and decide to watch it again. You place the DVD in the player, but there's something different. One short movie scene has been deleted – completely eliminated. And you rewind the movie and watch it again - but the scene is gone. You begin to wonder if it was ever there at all. You rewind the movie again, and watch it entirely. *Nothing.* You're now convinced the scene was never there at all. Over years of recollections regarding the movie, your new memory never includes the deleted scene," he stopped tapping his pen and smiled, convinced he made his point about repressed memories.

"I suspect this," he continued as he touched his finger to his lip, obviously thinking.

"I suspect the small chest or foot locker at your girlfriend's house had something in it which reminded you of your fathers military foot locker. Probably an odor," he paused again and looked at me as if waiting for an answer.

"Well, it smelled really strong when she opened it. Kind of musty," I recalled.

"And you said earlier you used to cover your face with your blanket as a child? When you would hide in your room?" he asked.

"Yes," I admitted, remembering years of hiding under the blanket as a small child.

"It was your safe place?" he asked.

"Yes," I responded, somewhat frustrated he wanted to rehash what we had already spoken of.

He tapped his finger on his lip.

"You lived in Los Angeles?" he asked.

"Oceanside at the time, by the military base. Say, closer to San Diego," I responded.

"A very warm climate none the less," he stated.

I nodded, "Yes sir."

"Did you have the same bedding for the summer and winter? Not that there's much of a winter in San Diego," he asked.

I slumped into the comfort of the couch cushion. I pulled my hood from behind my shoulders, and onto my head. I looked up at the ceiling and thought. The summers in Oceanside were very hot, and I spent a lot of time at the beach. When it was winter, it was warm, but not hot. At night, it would get cold. When it was cold I always slept with my blanket that had the fighter jets on it. We kept the blanket in...

"My father kept the blankets in a foot locker, in the garage. We would get them out in the fall," I blurted as soon as I recalled the memory of it.

"Mothballs," he stated.

"Excuse me?" I asked, confused at his statement.

I sat up from my seated position and pulled my hood from my head.

"Mothballs. It's very common for people in warmer climates to use mothballs when storing clothes and fabrics in a chest or locker. It prevents moths from eating the fabric in the off season. Your childhood blanket you covered your face with – the one you used as *protection* - it probably smelled of mothballs. Yesterday, when the chest at the foot of the bed was opened, the odor of mothballs resurrected the memories your mind had repressed for two decades. Odor is a strong trigger," he said as he dropped the pen onto his desk.

I sat and thought about what he had said. I didn't immediately feel better knowing *why* I had recalled the memories, but it was reassuring to know what had happened.

Mothballs.

"If I may, let's take this a step further," he said as he picked his pen up from the desk.

"Your hooded sweatshirt. You wear it at all times. At least during all seasons. I *do* realize you remove it," he chuckled.

"The hooded sweatshirt has become your safety blanket - the one from childhood. You wear it to hide from what it is you're uncertain of. Maybe what you want to protect yourself from. You wear it as superman wears his cape. It's a conscious decision you make with subconscious benefits. The hooded sweatshirt, in a sense, has assisted you in the repression of those memories. Have you been wearing hooded sweatshirts for a long time?" he stopped tapping his pen and waited for a response.

I thought again about California, my father, and my grandfather. I didn't remember wearing a hoodie in Oceanside. When I moved to Compton, I always had one. When we moved to Escondido for a while I had one, after mom was gone. From as best I could recall, I wore one from when we lived in Escondido until present time.

"I think I started wearing one when we lived in Escondido. I was around ten years old, I think – maybe eleven," I responded, finding his entire routine interesting.

"Was your mother in Escondido, or was she already gone?" he asked.

"Gone," I responded.

"Do you remember sleeping in a hooded sweatshirt?" he asked.

I scrunched my brow, finding this question odd. I thought about it as I sat up in the couch.

Is this asshole a doctor or a fucking detective?

"Yes, I guess so. I remember sleeping in it at my grandfather's house. And now that I'm thinking about it, I remember wearing a hoodie at the house that had the orange trees, and that was in Escondido, by the highway," I responded.

"Your hooded sweatshirt replaced your childhood blanket. You more than likely associated the blanket with your father's abuse of your mother. When your mother left and you moved to a new house, your means of *protection* changed. You began to hide inside your hood, not the blanket. You consciously gave up the blanket, and your subconscious received the eventual benefit," he smiled again.

This guy was good.

Putting all of the pieces together was a huge help, and I began to feel much better knowing what happened and why. It didn't change my anger toward my father for the abuse of my mother, but I felt it helped me tremendously.

"I suppose you're right, this is interesting," I said as I leaned back into the seat and crossed my legs.

"You mentioned your grandfather earlier, but you did not mention a grandmother. Was your grandmother around during your childhood?" he leaned back into his chair and placed his hands behind his head.

"No, they were divorced," I responded.

Silence.

No, surely not. My grandfather was one of the best men who ever existed. He was a saint. He was like a father to me. He taught me how to box, how to fight, how to channel my anger away from the streets and into the ring. He was a boxer. He was just like me, he was...

"If I may," he said after a few moments silence.

I uncrossed my legs, and crossed my arms in front of my chest. I nodded my head.

"When did you start boxing? Training to box?" he asked.

"When I was eleven, give or take," I responded.

"And you said earlier that your grandfather was your trainer and manager – until he died, correct?" he remained leaning back in his chair.

I nodded, "Yes sir."

"I believe you channeled your anger toward your father through the boxing. Your anger at the entire *situation*. Your mother leaving, your exposure to her beatings, your developed hatred toward abusers of women," he said calmly.

"I believe so, yes. I've always said I have demons inside of me. I suppose all of what we're talking about now is what has fueled me for years," I admitted.

"So, boxing allowed you to repress the memories of your mother, your father and the situation? To channel the anger and hatred elsewhere?" he asked softly.

His voice was nice and calm. I found him very easy to talk to.

"Yes sir," I responded.

"And when your father came home from the war, you were happy to see him? You had no recollection of the beatings or abuse after you started boxing?" he asked.

"Yes, I was happy to see him. And no, I had no recollection of any abuse or beatings," I responded.

"Now, your grandfather. I imagine if he trained you, if he was your trainer *and* your manager, he must have had experience?" he asked, still leaning back in his chair.

"Yes, he was a champion. He won several titles," I responded quickly. I was proud of my grandfather.

He paused.

Silence.

"Wait a fucking minute, doc. What are you saying?" I snarled as I sat up in my seat.

He leaned forward and picked up his pen. "I'm not saying anything. What are you thinking, Shane?"

"Well, you stopped talking. I'm not stupid. You stop talking when you want me to think," I frowned back at him.

"And what, Shane, did you think?" he asked.

"Well, I think you wanted me to think my grandfather abused my grandmother," I said angrily.

"I didn't *want* you to think anything, Shane. I gave you time to think whatever it is your mind developed as a thought or series of thoughts," he said quietly.

"I don't like this game," I said as I pulled my hood onto my head.

"It's not a game. I'm trying to help you. I'm trying to help you in regard to your father. Anger can destroy you. I'm trying to help you understand some things," he looked at his watch.

"We're about finished for the day, may I continue?" he asked.

I rolled my eyes.

"Sure," I sighed.

"Your grandfather's era. They rarely got divorced. Married couples in those days typically worked through any and all problems. Marriage was perceived, back then, as being far more sacred and far more of a commitment. Considering all things, I suspect your father abused your mother. Now, your grandfather being a boxer, and the fact he was divorced," he paused and picked up the pen from the desk.

"He may have abused your grandmother," he held his hand in the air to prevent me from speaking and took a breath.

"I say this for one reason only. To give your father a reason for being the way he was. It wasn't necessarily his fault he acted the way that he did. When children are exposed to abuse, they either become abusers or they're like you – one hundred percent opposed to it. It's anyone's guess where people land. It's like the son or daughter of a raging alcoholic. Some become alcoholic, and some are so opposed to the thought of drinking they abstain from it for a life time," he paused and lowered his hand.

I thought about what he said.

"So you're thinking maybe my father grew up seeing his father doing what I witnessed my father doing – and he just ended up abusing instead of abstaining?" I rubbed my chin and looked around the room.

"It's a thought. It's possible. We'll never know," he responded.

It made sense. Everything he had said about my hoodie and when I started wearing it as a child. The fact my childhood blanket had been used for security of sorts; and it was kept in a footlocker full of mothballs. My grandfather and his devotion to boxing; maybe it was why he got me involved in boxing. It was possible, I suppose, he started boxing as an outlet after my grandmother left. Knowing and understanding these things didn't allow me to forgive my father for what he did, but it was beginning to help me understand.

As adults, we are a product of what we were exposed to as children. Generations of abuse breed generations of abusers. Until one person is strong enough to break the chain.

I'm strong enough.

I stood from the couch and pressed my jeans with my hands, removing the wrinkles. He stood from his chair and walked around his desk, a business card in his hand.

"Would you like to make another appointment for your next session?" he asked.

"No sir, I'm done here. I appreciate your help. I'll be fine," I pulled my hood over my head.

"Good luck in your upcoming fight, Mr. Dekkar. I'm here if you need me," he said as he handed me the business card.

I placed the business card in my pocket and turned to face the door. I inhaled a slow breath through my nose and exhaled out my mouth. I grabbed the door handle and slowly opened the door, knowing the fight was the farthest thing from my mind right now. We all fight our battles differently. I chose to fight mine in the ring. My father fought his in Afghanistan and Iraq. Kace fought her battle attempting to make a relationship work which was destined to lose. We fight to form ourselves into something or someone we wouldn't naturally become.

We fight to become stronger.

And the strength, ultimately, allows us to continue to fight.

And the fighting builds strength and provides us with experience until we are strong enough to stand on our own.

I slid my hand under my shirt and felt my chest. *Bare.* Bare of the dog tags I had always carried as a reminder of my father and his devotion to fight for what he believed to be just, right and moral. I walked through the lobby to the front door and opened it. Holding the door handle in my hand, I stood in the opening. I took a deep breath and looked out into the street. And I stepped out into the world with a mind full of new memories. Full of memories but free of the chains which have bound me for so many years.

I stepped out into the world.

Free.

KACE

Shane had been home from the hospital for three weeks. He seemed measurably different since returning from the hospital, in good ways. He was more loving, willing to spend time being lazy around the house with me, and had been taking time to cuddle and do girlish things with me.

It was entirely possible the hospital was something he needed for a long time. It was probably necessary to get his mind clear after losing his father and grandfather in such a short period of time. He never talked to me about the trip to my mother's house, passing out, the ambulance ride, or what the doctor told him during his stay in the hospital.

The afternoon after we left him in the hospital, he called from a restaurant and explained he was done with all of his medical tests. He said whenever we were ready Ripp and I could come get him. The day in the restaurant was the last we spoke of any of it.

I know something inside of him changed, because he had not worn his dog tags since the day he tore them off and dropped them on the floor at my mother's house. The dog tags were his life, his good luck charm, and his only real tie to his father. I think they might have caused part of the problem, because he tore them off right before he collapsed.

Initially, I didn't really know how to treat it, so I placed them on the kitchen counter for him to pick up whenever he was ready. That night, they were gone. He didn't wear them, but I knew he took them from the counter. The next day, while Shane was showering, I accidentally threw away my driver's license when I was cleaning out my wallet. As soon as I realized it, I dug through the trash to try and find it. When I did, I saw the chain in the trash. I reached in and pulled at the chain, and found the dog tags attached, wrapped in paper to hide them.

I put them away until he decided he wanted or needed them. I didn't want to mention them and make him upset if he didn't want to talk about it. I knew whatever reason he was upset had to do with his father, and right now his father is a delicate subject. I didn't want to upset Shane, not now. Not ever for that matter. For now, I just wanted to enjoy him the way he was.

"Babe, where are you?" he asked as he walked in the door.

"I'm in here," I answered from the living room.

He walked into the living room holding a sack in his hand. His boots were clean and polished, and he was wearing a new black hoodie.

"Look," he said as he held one foot forward for me to see.

"They're clean. They look good. I like your new hoodie," I said as I looked back and forth between the cooking channel and his clean boots.

"No, babe. They're *new*," he said.

"You bought new boots?" I asked as I turned off the television.

"Brand fucking new," he said.

He has changed.

"Holy cow. Where are the old ones?" I asked as I stood from the couch.

"Garage. I put 'em up. Got a new hoodie, too," he said as he slowly turned in a circle.

"I love it, it looks comfy. The old one?"

"Garage," he responded.

"Oh, wow. And how long had you been wearing those old boots?" I asked.

"Uhhm. Well, six. No, seven. Eight. Yeah, eight years," he responded.

"Wow," I said, glad that he finally replaced them.

He looked inside the sack he held, pulled out a receipt, and then handed it to me.

"There's a few dresses in there. Go in the bedroom and try them on for me," he smiled.

"You bought me dresses?" I asked as I eagerly grabbed the bag from his grasp.

As he nodded his head, he unzipped and removed his hoodie. I looked inside the bag. One dress was black and one was a burnt orange color. I loved getting gifts, and I love clothes. I hadn't received a gift for around ten years as far as I could remember. Holding the bag in my hand, I reached around his neck and hugged him.

"Thank you, I love you, Shane," I said.

"I love you. Now go try them on," he said as he sat on the couch and began to remove his boots.

"Can I come out and model them for you?" I asked as I walked to the room.

"Yes, that's what I want. I want you to try them on and come out here so I can see," he said as he shook his head.

This is so exciting.

I ran to the room and shut the door.

I held up the black dress. Black is elegant. *Boring.* I held up the orange dress. *Oh my, this is nice. It's going to look so good.* I got undressed and put on the orange dress and looked in the mirror. I looked fabulous.

Awesome sauce.

If I go out there in this one first, then the black one will be last, and I won't end it with a bang.

I took the orange dress off and put on the black one. I looked great, but I needed shoes. I opened the closet and dug for my favorite 4" heels. I found the heels and pulled them onto my feet. I stood and looked in the mirror.

Oh wow.

Wow.

I opened the drawer to my dresser and pulled out my perfume and one of my folded tee shirts. I sprayed the folded tee shirt with perfume, pulled up the dress, and rubbed the tee shirt under my chest.

That ought to do it.

I looked in the mirror and pulled my hair behind my ears the way he likes to see it.

Ok, here we go.

I grabbed the door handle and looked in the mirror.

I look too conservative.

As I turned the door handle, I shook my head and walked out into the living room.

"Don't move," he said as soon as I walked out of the bedroom.

"Why? What's wrong?" I asked, startled.

"Don't. Kace, don't move," he said as he stood up from the couch, "Take a step back by the door."

"What?" I asked as I stood a few steps into the living room.

"Just back up one or two steps, into the light," he said as he walked toward the kitchen.

Slowly, I stepped backward two steps.

"Right there, don't move," he said from the edge of the kitchen.

He grabbed his phone and started walking my direction. He stood a few feet in front of me and held his phone in front of him, looking at the screen. As I stood there smiling, he took a few pictures of me with his phone. He looked at the phone, scrolled through the pictures, and knelt down closer to the floor.

He took another picture and looked at the phone, "Perfect."

"Kace, you're as beautiful of a human being as has ever existed. Looking at you is proof there is a God, he pays attention to his work, and he appreciates it. I wonder what I have ever done to deserve having the ability to just come home to you every day," he said as he stood and stared at the screen of the phone.

"Look at this," he said as he held his phone in front of my face and stepped beside me.

I looked at the screen. The girl looking back at me was beautiful. Her hair was blonde and healthy looking. Wearing a new black dress and heels, she looked elegant. Her skin held on to the late summer tan, and was free of blemishes. As I studied the picture I realized Shane had changed me. He had made me confident. He gave me reason to believe I was beautiful. He asked me daily, several times, *who's the most beautiful girl in the world?*

He knew what he was doing.

Looking at the screen of the phone, I realized he was right.

I was beautiful.

And Shane knew it. Long before I realized it, he knew it. He brought it to my attention. He told me over and over, in his own way. And now he stood beside me showing me. He truly believed I was beautiful for all of this time, and now he was making sure I knew it. I tried to remember the last time I looked at a picture of myself. I couldn't even recall the last time. I had no reason to have pictures. Josh's rules really didn't let me take, send, or have a reason to need pictures.

"I could just look at you for a lifetime," Shane said as he looked up from the screen of the phone.

"Do it," I responded, "Do it."

"I intend to," he chuckled as he tossed the phone onto the floor.

"Want me to try on the other dress now?" I asked, standing there a little more confident than before.

"Take that one off, Kace," he said.

"Want to see the other one?" I asked again, excited to put on the other dress.

"Take it off, Kace. *Now.* Take it off. I can't take it any longer. Looking at you makes me realize you're real. Here's the thing, Kace. Every time I come home, every time I meet you for lunch, every time I wake up and look over at you," he paused and placed his hands on either side of my face.

He held my face and looked into my eyes, "You're more beautiful than I ever remember you being."

I melted into a puddle.

"Kace, every time I go somewhere with you, I hold my head high. Proud you're stepping down to my level. I'm surprised someone like you would even be with someone like me. I stand beside you proudly, hopeful I can make you a fraction as happy as you make me. I love you, Kace," he said as he kissed me softly.

As he pulled away from my lips, he focused on my face, "Off, Kace.

Now."

"Okay, I'll go grab the other one," I sighed, still full of emotion from his little speech.

"No," he said as he grabbed my shoulders and turned me around.

I felt him unzip the zipper of the dress. The dress fell to the floor. He knelt down at my feet, removed my shoes one at a time, and tossed the dress to the side. Dressed in my panties and bra, he led me by my hand into the bedroom.

A certain satisfaction filled me as we walked into the room. I was satisfied Shane cared for me enough to buy me gifts and remind me I was beautiful. I'm further satisfied he loved me – and he accepted my love in return. As we reached the bed, he turned me around and lowered my body onto it. Slowly, I allowed myself to fall to the bed. His fingers slid to my panties, pulling them along my thighs. I raised my feet and kicked my legs to free my panties from my feet.

I sat up slightly and reached back to unhook my bra as he pulled his shirt over his head. As he reached to unbuckle his belt, his bicep muscles flexed and twitched. He stood at the end of the bed as he removed his jeans and looked like an absolute God.

Shane Dekker was the sweetest man I had ever met. He was also the most brutal man to ever enter the boxing ring. He was now, and would always remain the most gorgeous man I have even seen in my life. His innocence and shy nature did nothing but added to the fact he was as tough as almost anyone on earth – it made him even more attractive. It made him human. Soon he may be fighting for the Heavyweight Champion in the World title. Looking at him stand before me made it almost difficult to believe.

As I tossed my bra to the floor, I wiped the drool from my lips.

Now standing naked, he inched his way beside me on the bed. Shane knew by now all I had to do was see him without a shirt, listen to him speak, or watch him get undressed and I was as wet as I would ever become.

"Babe?" he whispered.

I turned my head to face him. As our eyes met, he began to kiss me. As he kissed me his hands touched the sides of my face lightly. He touched my face almost every time we kissed, and it drove me insane with emotion. It was the one thing which always pushed me over the edge.

His soft lips against mine, I moaned as he kissed me. One of his hands left my face and began to massage my breasts. He began to roll my nipple between his index finger and thumb. An electrical charge felt as if it were traveling from my nipple to my aching pussy.

Foreplay with Shane Dekker wasn't foreplay at all, it was torture.

He moved his mouth from my lips to the edge of my neck. As he drug his teeth down the side of my neck, I felt goose bumps rise from my calf to my shoulder. His lips began to kiss my collar bone and work their way back up my neck to my jaw.

My entire body felt as if it were on fire.

As he kissed my jaw and worked his way down to my chin, his hands found my breasts. I closed my eyes and focused on his mouth. My breasts cupped in each of his hands, he started squeezing them as he kissed my chin and neck. He opened his mouth wide and began kissing the front of my neck. I arched my back and tilted my head back, exposing my neck for his pleasure.

As he licked and kissed my neck, he began to moan.

No, don't do that.

Don't moan.

I opened my eyes.

The muscles on the backs of his arms flexed as he squeezed my breasts. His perfectly flat stomach was against my hips and mid-section as he kissed the side of my face and chin. I watched his chest muscles as he kissed up and down my neck.

I reached down and fumbled for his cock. As I gripped it in my hand, he began to groan.

"Oh God, Kace," he moaned as he raised his mouth from my chin.

"Lay down," I said, "Lay on your back."

I pushed against his shoulder, forcing him to roll to his back. As he did, I kissed my way along his body toward his waist.

"Don't move. Let me do this for you, please," I begged.

I kissed his neck and worked my way to his chest. Knowing I could not last for very long, I bit each of his nipples and moved to the center of his torso. I rubbed my hands along his washboard abs as I kissed along his stomach. Holding my hands on his stomach, I moved my mouth to his hard cock.

"Hold my hair so it doesn't get in my mouth," I said.

Silently, he reached for my hair and held it behind my head. I opened my mouth and began to lick the tip of his cock. As I licked and kissed the tip, I moved my hand from his stomach and grabbed his cock in my hand.

I pulled my mouth away from the tip and watched as I began to stroke his cock. Being able to do things like this was very pleasurable to me. I had never been in a position where I was allowed or able to enjoy myself sexually. Shane's fear of causing me harm or emotional damage prevented him from being aggressive with me sexually, and I was able to show him through my actions what I preferred and enjoyed.

It was a learning experience for both of us each time we had sex.

"I like your cock in my hand," I said as I stroked it.

I sat up on the bed and began to stroke it faster. I leaned over and slid my mouth down the shaft as far as I could a few times, making the entire length wet. I pulled my mouth from the tip and began stroking it again.

"But," I said as I raised myself from the bed and stepped over his thighs.

I like it in *here* better.

I lowered myself onto his hard cock as I spread my pussy open with my fingers. As the tip penetrated me, I had a light orgasm. I sighed and lowered myself slowly down until I had his entire cock inside of me. Once down as far as I could go, I wiggled my ass against his upper thighs.

"See? All gone," I said as I proudly pointed to my pussy.

I leaned forward and placed my hands on each side of his chest and took a deep breath. I raised myself up the shaft of his cock until my pussy was at the rim of the tip. I bit my lip and lowered myself down the shaft until it was buried inside of me.

I exhaled.

"Did you see that?" I asked.

He nodded eagerly.

"You do realize this doesn't hurt me, right?"

I rose up again, almost to the tip.

"See that," I said as I pointed to his glistening cock.

He nodded, "Yeah, fuck yeah I do."

I dropped myself down the length of his stiff cock and gasped as it bottomed out.

I pointed to my soaking wet pussy, "Gone. See that? Gone."

I worked my way up slowly. As I did, he propped himself onto his elbows and leaned forward to watch.

"Your cock is huge. I fucking love it. Pay attention, because I'm going to fuck you, Shane. I'm going to see how I like this. I'll let you know," I smiled.

I began working my hips as quickly and ferociously as I could. My pussy was beyond soaked. His cock worked in and out of my wet pussy as quickly as I could fuck it. My only limitation was what little friction there was, and there wasn't much, because the wetness from my pussy was running down his cock onto his hips. With my hands on his chest I began to moan and scream.

"You...."

"Don't....Oh fucking God."

"Make me nervous," I breathed.

"Because I fucking," I bucked my hips up and down, swallowing his cock inside of me with each stroke.

"Not nervous...Because I...Love you," I said.

"Holy shit, I'm gonna cum," I continued rocking my hips slowly, taking all of him inside me.

Almost as if he were in a trance, He stared at my pussy, watching each stroke as my ass and pussy rose up from his lap.

"I love your....okay....I'm gonna cum now," I gasped.

I closed my eyes as they rolled back in my head. I felt myself begin to climax as I focused on the feeling of his thick cock inside of me. My entire body shook as I came all over Shane's cock. I held my body still and pressed on his chest, sitting on him with my eyes closed.

His hands reached up and touched my hips. As soon as his fingers touched me, I jumped.

"Are you okay, babe?" he asked.

"Yeah, don't touch me," I said, before I really knew what I was saying.

"Don't touch you? Are you okay? Did I hurt you?" he asked quietly.

I raised my hands from his chest and waved my arms in front of him.

"Shhhh. Don't talk to me. Don't touch me," I laughed.

I was in some post-climax bliss. My entire body was tingling, and when he touched me it sent a tingly shock throughout my body. It was just too much for me to take. I needed more practice. Fucking Shane was so much different. So much more enjoyable. Right now, I needed to recover and come back to earth.

Silence.

I wanted the feeling, forever. The right here. The right now. I wanted to bask in it for a lifetime. The feeling was what my books were written about. Everyone wants this and no one actually gets it. I was in heaven.

This is life with Shane Dekkar.

"Babe you're shaking," he said as his hand touched my thigh.

"Don't talk," I said as I opened my eyes.

He looked up at me, his face filled with worry.

"I need a minute," I said.

His eyes widened.

I closed my eyes, "It's good, babe. The good kind of *don't talk to me*. The good kind of don't touch me. The, *oh my God, I want this feeling to last forever* type of feeling. That's what I've got going on."

I paused and took a slow, deep breath.

"It's okay, I'm fine now. You can talk," I said as I slid back on his thighs toward his knees.

"What happened?" he asked.

I shrugged my shoulders and looked at him in amazement.

"*You* happened, Shane. You happened," I responded, still in a daze.

Slowly, he smiled.

"You knew you were going to do this to me, didn't you?" I asked.

He tapped me once on the thigh.

"Fucker," I smiled.

"Kace, I didn't *ask* for this. I wasn't looking for a girlfriend. I wasn't trying to find a partner, a wife, a whatever. All I know is this – you entered my life, and when you did, things changed. Things inside of me changed. The feelings you cause me to feel, they're different. They're not like other feelings I have ever had. Now that I have felt *this*, I know what everyone talks about. I know what it's like to feel as if you *need* someone to just survive. It scares me. *You* scare me," he said as he sat up in the bed.

"I scare you? Seriously?" I slid off of his legs and lay down beside him, my head resting on my hand.

"The good kind," he chuckled, now sitting straight up in the bed.

"I don't *need*. I never have. I have always been fine being alone. I've always known it's how I'd live my life, I suppose - alone and happy. Now that I've met you - now that we have *this* - I can't deny it's meant to be. Kace, I'm scared to death to try and live without you," he said.

I looked into his eyes and felt full of emotion. I felt full of pride. Full of love. I was about to cry, and I don't like to cry.

"You'll never be without me, Shane. Never," I said as I rubbed his arm with my free hand.

"Never?" he asked.

"Never," I responded.

He made a fist and held it over his chest.

I made a fist and tapped it against his clenched hand.

"You're stuck now," he said.

"How so?" I asked.

"We just shook on it," he said.

And the way Shane's mind works…

We just became one.

SHANE

"You think he's ready, Mike?" Kelsey asked.

"I'm ready," I said as I set my water down on the table.

Kelsey turned his head to face me and scrunched his brow, "I wasn't talking to you. I was talking to Mike."

"Mean face," Kace laughed.

Kelsey looked at Kace and scowled as Ripp put his beer on the table and inhaled deeply.

"Well, I ain't saying this because he's sitting here, you know me better than that. I can say I've watched all the videos. I've studied this guy Mc Claskey, and if he does what we've been practicing," Ripp nodded his head my direction.

"That guy ain't got a fucking chance. Dekk's gonna slaughter him," Ripp finished.

"Well, we can't go into this thinking we got it in the bag. It damned sure isn't gonna be easy. It's gonna be a bitch, you hear me?" Kelsey said as he turned to face me.

"A bitch boss," I said.

"God damn it, I ain't fucking kidding. You two arrogant assholes," Kelsey said as he pressed his hands against the table and flexed his forearms.

"Flexin' on me boss?" I chuckled.

"Get the ticket, I'm buying," Kelsey said as he let go of the table.

"Kace ain't done eating yet," Ripp said as he pointed to Kace, who was just starting to eat her salad.

"Don't mean I can't pay. Now you're gonna be there, right? I need you to be there," Kelsey said toward Kace.

"I'm his cheerleader," Kace responded in between bites.

"And you'll be there?" Kelsey said as he nodded his head toward Kace again.

"Damn, Kelsey," I complained.

"I need her to *say* it," he said.

"Yes sir. I will be there," Kace responded as she made a fist with her hand.

She held her fist over the table toward Kelsey. Kelsey turned and looked toward Ripp and then directly at me.

"Don't look at *me*," I said.

"I got this," Kace laughed, shaking her fist over the center of the table.

"Do it," Ripp said toward Kelsey.

Kelsey made a fist and reached toward Kace. As she bumped her fist sharply against his she shook her head, flipping her hair over her shoulder.

"It's settled," she said, "We shook on it."

"What do you think about the title fight, boss? If I win?" I asked.

"Shit, that's in the bag," Ripp responded.

"He's right," Kelsey said as he nodded his head toward Ripp, "If you win this fight, you'll be a shoe-in for the Heavyweight Championship fight. All we'll have to do is ask. For him not to fight you would be suicide for his career. This is it, kid. This is *the* fight," Kelsey said.

"What did I tell you about that *kid* shit," I laughed.

Kelsey had been calling me kid since the day we met. At first, it bothered me, and now it was just part of Kelsey being Kelsey. He did it to try to drive me, to build my spirit, and to give me the inner anger I needed to fight. He didn't realize it, but there was no need to call me names. It didn't give me reason to fight. My reason was inside of my soul, my inner demons. This was *who* I was, not something developed from taunting or teasing.

"I want the title. I want to get the title, and then…" I thought about trying to fight for the title, and what I would do if I won.

Retire undefeated, holding the Heavyweight Championship belt?

Defend the title?

Take the pay-off and spend a lifetime of being happy with Kace?

Have kids?

"And then?" Ripp asked as he finished drinking his beer, "then what?"

I turned and looked at Kace, as if she held the answer. I looked at Kelsey as he raised one eyebrow.

"We're going to defend that motherfucker, aren't we kid?" Kelsey said.

I shrugged my shoulders, not really knowing the answer. I had to win the fight on the table now, it was first. Other than fighting Ripp, I hadn't had a fight since I fought Wilson. Not that Ripp was less of a fighter than anyone else I could find, but fighting Ripp was different.

It was easy for me to fight Ripp. Getting in the ring with him was like going to work. I knew what to expect before, during, and after the fight. As great as the sparring had been between us, and as much as I appreciated the fact he had helped train me for the last few months, I wondered.

"We've got to win this fight first, boss. Let's focus on this one right now," I responded.

"Done," Kace said as she proudly shoved her empty plate to the center of the table.

"You eat like a girl," Kelsey laughed.

"I *am* a girl," Kace responded as she reached for her glass of water.

"I normally don't like women around my fighters before a fight. They need to go into these things cock strong. You seem to give Shane strength. I like that," Kelsey said.

"What's cock strong?" Kace asked.

Ripp and I chuckled, neither really wanting to answer her question.

Ripp turned to Kace and smiled, "It's when...well...what he means is *this*. It's when a fighter or a player goes the entire length of time before a fight or a big game without getting any *relief*. Without getting any..."

"Pussy," he whispered.

Kace turned toward me and then slowly rotated her head to face Kelsey. She locked her eyes on his. Slowly, she leaned forward on the table and rested on her elbows on the edge. As she lowered her chin into her hands, she smiled.

"Too late," she said very matter-of-factly.

"Are you fucking serious?" Kelsey cried, turning from facing Kace to facing me.

Without an immediate response, he turned to look at Ripp. Ripp shrugged his shoulders and stood up.

"Ready?" Ripp asked.

"Yep," I responded as I stood up, "Let's get."

Still seated, Kelsey turned to face Kace; who remained in her seat, as she was when she spoke to Kelsey a moment before. Kelsey leaned his elbows on the table to mimic Kace, and placed his chin in his hands.

Ripp stood up and pushed his hands into his pockets.

Kelsey and his superstitious beliefs. It was too late to correct it now. Kelsey would be certain to blame Kace if the fight was lost. In his mind, my having sex preceding the fight would be a definite way to seal a loss. I had never dreamed sex would come up in conversation; or I wouldn't have brought Kace to the pre-fight dinner.

"Seriously?" Kelsey asked again, staring directly into Kace's eyes.

"No," she chuckled as she remained focused on Kelsey.

"I know better than to fuck a man before a fight. Even if he asked me, I'd tell him no. I want him to win this more than you do," she said as she made a fist and held it in the center of the table.

Kelsey made a fist and smacked it against hers sharply, "I like this girl, kid. She's got spunk."

You have no idea. I thought.

You have no idea.

KACE

Something about watching two men fight each other in a confined space was very exciting to me. I never would have guessed it would be something I would enjoy; but I doubt after seeing a boxing match for my first time there's any one event which would ever satisfy me more. The two men covered in sweat, the fighting, the arena full of adrenaline, and the fact one of the two men was my boyfriend was enough to make me an excited wet mess for the entire fight and many hours afterward.

Watching. Men. Fight. Makes. Me. Wet.

Part of the problem with Shane's fights was they never lasted that long.

"There he is Ripp. Here he comes," I jumped up and down and pointed as Shane came up the aisle toward the ring.

Watching Shane walk, in general, excited me. Seeing Shane walk into *this* crowd was the most excited I had ever been in my life. The fight was an undercard fight for the championship, and was televised on pay television. If Shane won, he will be offered a fight for the Heavyweight Championship of the World - the equivalent of the Super Bowl for boxers.

"Damn he looks good, Shorty. These fuckin' seats are the shit. Ringside, fuck yeah," Ripp said as pulled me close to him.

"Mc Claskey's a fucking punk!" Ripp screamed toward Shane when he walked by.

Shane turned and looked our direction for a brief second, nodded his head and winked. Kelsey turned and scowled, probably aggravated that we would break Shane's concentration on his way to the ring. Kelsey was a very superstitious man, and he wanted Shane to win the fight more than Shane did.

"Fuck You Kelsey!" Ripp screamed through his cupped hands.

Ripp was obviously as excited as I was. He was a great fighter, but he didn't fight as often as Shane did. He fought lower rate fighters, and other than the fight with Shane, had never been beaten. He had never taken the time to have a good manager, trainer, or fighting schedule. He enjoyed having the title of being undefeated, but really wasn't willing to take many chances to risk losing it.

"How much longer? Is this like any other match?" I was so excited I could barely contain myself.

"Just a little more bullshit because it's a televised fight It'll be going here in just a minute or two," Ripp responded as he waved his fists.

Our seats were ringside seats. They were in the front, right beside the ring, and close to the aisle Shane walked down to get to the ring. Our position would allow us to see all of the action almost like we were standing in the ring.

"Ladies and gentlemen….." the announcer said into the microphone.

I felt almost sick. I realized I was still standing, and had never sat down. I looked at Ripp, who was also standing. This was becoming very real. Cameras were everywhere filming the event from every angle.

"*In the blue corner. Shane,*" the announcer paused.

"*Shame on,*" he paused again and looked both directions.

"*Dehhhhhkkaaaaarrrr,*" he said the last name very slow and strung out.

"You got this, Dekk. You fucking got this!" Ripp screamed.

"*And, in the red corner,*" the announcer started.

"That son-of-a-bitch is bigger than I am. God damn. He's fucking huge," Ripp whispered my direction as the announcer was speaking.

I turned to Ripp, "Shane's gonna be okay, right?"

"Yeah, he'll be fine. Dekk's mean as a god damned snake, Shorty. Meanest mother fucker I ever met. Don't forget that. The man he becomes in the ring. You don't know that man. And you don't want to," Ripp responded.

"Shane's gonna be okay though?" I asked.

"Shorty, he'll be fine. I've seen him in street fights and in the ring. Nobody's going to beat him. When he walks into a fight, he flips a switch. He *becomes* a fighter, not some ordinary man who's boxing. The devil's blood pumps through him," Ripp reassured me.

"Okay," I turned back toward the ring.

"*Ding!*"

"Here we go," Ripp screamed.

Shane immediately went to the center of the ring. The other fighter circled around him. Shane threw a few punches toward Mc Claskey's face. The impact of the gloves made a thud as they hit the fighter's face and body.

Shane and Mc Claskey exchanged punches back and forth like they were in a punching contest, just trading punches back and forth in turns.

"C'mon Dekk, you can't brawl with this big prick, he's too strong. Use your speed," Ripp screamed toward the ring.

"What's happening?" I asked.

Ripp turned to face me, "He's brawling. Just toe-to-toe fighting this big bastard. Mc Claskey will kill him. He's too fucking big. Dekk's gotta box his ass. Out think him."

"Ten seconds, Dekk," Ripp screamed.

Ding!

"My stomach hurts," I said as soon as Shane walked back toward the corner of the ring.

"Mine too, that's ten-nine Mc Claskey for sure," Ripp said as he shook his head.

"God damn it, Dekk. Use your speed," Ripp screamed toward the ring.

"Shane didn't do good?" I asked.

"No Shorty, he didn't. He might just be feeling this guy out. Seeing what his style is. He's fighting southpaw, and this guy's leftie too. We talked about it, and this guy doesn't fight lefties very well. He does better against right handed fighters. But he can't just stand and fight this big fucker. He'll kill Dekk," Ripp explained.

I knew southpaw meant left handed in boxer slang. But Ripp said Shane would be fine. I didn't like the thought of Shane getting hurt. I reached into my pocket and rubbed Shane's dog tags. I had brought them for good luck, and didn't tell Ripp or Shane. I knew how they were all superstitious about certain things.

"You said he'd be fine, Ripp," I turned to Ripp and said softly.

"Not if he keeps this up. But it's only the first round," Ripp responded.

My stomach was in knots. I wanted this to be over. Thinking of Shane losing was sad, but the thought of him being hurt was something I could not even fathom.

Kelsey put Shane's mouthpiece back into his mouth and looked like he was scolding him. Kelsey had stood and screamed at Shane for most of the first round. I wondered if he was mad at Shane, or if this was something trainers did in the big fights to encourage a fighter to fight harder. According to Ripp, Shane became the devil in the ring. Nobody should be able to beat the devil. Not in a boxing match.

Ding!

Shane immediately went to the center of the ring, and Mc Claskey pushed him and punched him toward the corner of the ring.

"Stay out of that corner. He'll kill ya', Dekk," Ripp screamed.

Within a few seconds Mc Claskey had Shane in the corner, smashing him against the ropes. Shane's hands were covering his face, and the other fighter was swinging his fists wildly into Shane's arms and stomach. Seeing him beaten like this was very difficult for me.

"Push him off, god damn it, Dekk. Get outta the corner," Ripp screamed.

Mc Claskey's feet shuffled, and Shane pushed against him. At the same time, Shane swiveled his body and moved around Mc Claskey. As he did, he went to the center of the ring and began to bounce up and down on his feet.

Thank God.

My heart started racing as soon as Shane got out of the corner. Mc Claskey was now in the center of the ring, pushing against Shane with his fists held up against his face. As he pushed against Shane with his forearms, Shane swung wildly into his mid-section and threw a few wild uppercuts that missed.

"Get him baby!" I screamed.

I slapped Ripp's shoulder and squealed, "He's getting him, Ripp. He's getting him."

Mc Claskey swung a punch up into Shane's jaw, and it forced his head back sharply. Shane stumbled, and as soon as he did, I heard Ripp.

"Oh, god damn," Ripp mumbled.

"What?' I turned toward Ripp.

"Oh fuck," Ripp responded as he stared at the ring.

His hands quickly covered his mouth. I turned back to the fight. Mc Claskey jabbed toward Shane, hitting him directly in the face as Shane was stepping away from him. As soon as the punch hit Shane, he went down to the mat.

"Oh my God. Oh my God, Ripp. He's hurt!" I screamed.

Seeing Shane down on the mat was unsettling to me. I didn't think Shane has ever been knocked down, ever. He says, *never been down and never been out*, which means he's never been knocked down and never been knocked out. He's undefeated for a reason. Shane was better than this, something was wrong. I reached in my pocket, closed my eyes, and rubbed the dog tags again.

Please, God. Make Shane see what he always sees. Make him understand what to do to keep from getting hurt. I am not asking you to have him win this fight. All I want, Lord, is for you to make him understand what he always understands. Make him see what he always sees. I love him Lord, don't let him get hurt or die.

Amen.

"Good, thank God," Ripp said as he pulled his hands from his mouth.

"What?" I asked as Shane quickly stood up.

"See how the referee waved his hands?" he asked as he pointed toward the ring.

I hadn't seen it, but I agreed, "Yeah."

"The Referee ruled it a *slip*, not a knockdown. Thank God. If this goes to the cards, that'd kill him," Ripp whispered.

"Oh. Good," I whispered back.

"Get him babe," I screamed.

Shane was covered in sweat and his arm muscles were flexing each time he threw a swing or got close to the other fighter and defended himself. Seeing him hit the other fighter was exciting and made me wish he would start doing better. This Mc Claskey guy was huge and I didn't like him beating on Shane.

Ding!

As soon as Shane came to the corner, Kelsey started yelling at him. Kelsey screamed at Shane the entire break. He even hit Shane's arm a few times as he screamed. He turned and pointed toward Ripp and I a few times as he screamed at Shane. I didn't like seeing Kelsey or Shane like this.

The third round and the start of the fourth round were just like the first two rounds. Shane and Mc Claskey traded punches, and there was no real progress made by Shane toward winning. A few times, Mc Claskey got Shane into the corner. According to Ripp, it's impossible to get Shane in the corner. Ripp said something was wrong with Shane. I wondered about what had changed since Shane's last fight.

The dog tags.

This was the first fight he hadn't had the dog tags during a fight.

He doesn't know they're here.

Maybe he needs to know I brought them.

Or.

I considered maybe my being selfish and bringing the dog tags to the fight was causing him lose. Maybe he didn't want them for a reason. I began to wonder if my bringing the dog tags was causing Shane to fight poorly. As the fourth round was coming close to the end, I considered walking to the trash barrel by the ring and throwing them away. I looked up at the fight. As Shane stepped from the corner, Mc Claskey swung a wild punch toward Shane. The punch caught Shane's shoulder as he was stepping away, and Shane went down to the mat again.

"It was a slip, Ref, it was a fucking slip," Ripp screamed.

I screeched as Shane hit the mat. The referee waved his arms, ruling it a slip.

"Oh shit, Kelsey's hollering for me. I'll be right back," Ripp said as he stepped out of his seat and walked to the corner of the ring.

Ripp and Kelsey talked as Shane and Mc Claskey traded punches. Kelsey screamed at Ripp, pointed at Shane, and pointed at me. I could not tell what he was screaming about, but he seemed very angry. Ripp came back to his seat looking frantic.

"Kelsey wants us to find someone with dog tags, Shorty. We need to find someone with dog tags quick. Kelsey needs to try and get Shane invested in this fight, and he thinks Shane not having his dog tags is the difference," Ripp pleaded as he looked around the arena.

I swallowed a lump in my throat.

"I have Shane's dog tags," I said as I reached into my pocket.

"*The* dog tags?" he asked.

I nodded, somewhat embarrassed, "Yes, I dug them out of the trash."

"Holy fuck. C'mon," he demanded as he grabbed my arm.

As we started walking toward Kelsey, I pulled the dog tags from my pocket. Ripp took me right to the corner by Kelsey. I was embarrassed and filled with shame.

"Boss, she's got Dekk's dog tags. *The* tags," Ripp said as he grabbed my wrist, holding my hand up for Kelsey to see.

SCOTT HILDRETH

"Praise the fucking Lord. Alright, listen to me," he demanded as he grabbed my face with his hands.

"Fucking listen," he screamed at me as the bell sounded.

Ding!

"We've got one fucking minute, *you've* got about thirty seconds of that minute. Say something meaningful to him. And God damn it Kace, make it count," he growled.

Kelsey released my face and turned toward the ring. I looked up as Shane came to the corner. Kelsey screamed at Shane and Shane spit in the bucket. He gave Shane water from the bottle and I stepped toward the ring with the dog tags in my hand.

"Hey kid, lookie here," Kelsey said as he stepped to Shane's side and pointed toward me.

"Shane," I said quietly, attempting to get Shane's attention.

Without thinking, I held the dog tags behind my back and started talking. I let my mind and my mouth just flow, saying whatever came to mind. For once in my life, what I thought, felt, and said were the same. Nothing got jumbled, and everything just came out.

"Your father fought his demons in the war, Shane. He made peace with himself, God, and probably your mother before or maybe just as he died. He fought in that war to make everything that was jumbled up inside his head make some kind of sense. You fight your demons in the boxing ring, babe. You wore these dog tags for years as a tribute to your father. The person he was hasn't changed. It's just your perception, Shane. He *chose* to fight in the war. He volunteered. He did it to make you proud of him. Now, it's your turn. Do your god damned job. Make *him* proud."

I moved my hand from behind my back, producing the dog tags. I

225

dangled them in front of Shane as I began to cry.

Sitting on his stool, Shane glanced at Ripp, turned toward Kelsey, and pounded his fists together; holding the dog tags between his gloves. Kelsey reached toward Shane's mouth with the mouthpiece. Shane shook his head and released the dog tags into my hands.

"I got this," he said toward Ripp and me.

He turned to Kelsey, "My way."

Kelsey shoved the mouthpiece into Shane's mouth as the bell rang.

Shane jumped up and shuffled to the center of the ring.

Ripp and I hurried back to our seats. As we got into place, Ripp turned to face me.

"You damn near had me in tears, Shorty. You did real well. Now, hold those things tight in your hand," he motioned to the dog tags hanging from the chain in my hand.

I gripped the dog tags and turned to face the ring, Shane was fighting in close with Mc Claskey. Mc Claskey was pounding Shane just like in the other rounds – beating his mid-section and arms. Mc Claskey swung a wild uppercut and missed Shane's chin by an inch as Shane leaned away from the punch.

Mc Claskey worked Shane into the corner and began clenching him – almost hugging him as they pressed against the ropes in the corner of the ring. Both fighters were covered in sweat, their muscles twitching as they pressed against each other and threw the occasional punch.

"He's tired, Shorty. That big fucker's tired, he's clenching him. Dekk's no fool," Ripp screamed as he pointed to the corner where they were fighting.

"Get out of that corner, Dekk. He's worn out already," Ripp screamed.

Shane began twisting his body, attempting to break free from between Mc Claskey and the ropes. As Mc Claskey stepped back, Shane broke free, and Mc Claskey fell into the ropes. Shane immediately went to the center of the ring, leaving Mc Claskey at the corner.

Mc Claskey turned, and began to work his way slowly to the center of the ring. As he did, Shane pounded his fists together and curled his gloves toward his chest repeatedly.

"Oh shit," Ripp laughed.

"He's taunting him," he said as he pointed at the ring.

"He's calling him out. That's like a slap in the face," Ripp chuckled.

"C'mon, Dekk!" Ripp screamed.

As soon as Mc Claskey got close enough to Shane to swing, he threw a punch. Shane moved his head to the right, and the punch flew past his head. My heart began to race. As soon as Mc Claskey pulled his hand back, Shane shuffled his feet, and began dancing around Mc Claskey, curling his gloves.

"What the fuck?" Ripp said.

"What?" I asked.

"Well, look. He's switching it up. He's switched to orthodox. He's gonna fight him orthodox. What the fuck's he doing?" Ripp kind of chuckled as he spoke.

I knew that orthodox meant right handed. Shane could fight both ways, and depending on who he was fighting, would train to fight one way or the other. He had trained to fight this fight left handed - switching his style in the middle of the fight was not normal.

Kelsey began screaming toward the center of the ring.

Mc Claskey worked his way toward Shane. As he approached, Shane hit him in the face and shoulders with a series of quick jabs. Mc Claskey began to raise his gloves, and as soon as he did, Shane hit him in the stomach.

Mc Claskey's face looked like he'd been shot. Obviously Shane got him with a good one. Shane continued to pummel Mc Claskey's torso with punches and would swing an uppercut every few punches.

Ripp started screaming.

The entire crowd started to stand up and cheer.

Mc Claskey threw a few short punches and attempted to clutch Shane, holding him in close. Shane pushed his gloves against Mc Claskey and stepped back, freeing himself from his grasp. Immediately, as they separated, Shane hit Mc Claskey with a series of punches – initially to the mid-section and then to the face and shoulders. A wild uppercut barely missed. Mc Claskey offered little if anything in return.

The crowd continued to roar.

Shane stepped back. Mc Claskey approached. As he did, Shane hit him with left and right jabs in the face. As Mc Claskey raised his gloves to his face, Shane hit his gloves. Some of the fans began chanting. I tried to block them out and stay focused on the fight. Shane began to work Mc Claskey's mid-section harder and harder, hitting him two dozen times to Mc Claskey's two or three. As soon as Mc Claskey would attempt to fight back, Shane would step aside or away. Mc Claskey seemed to become tired.

Shane was winning now, and my view of the fight changed completely. This was exciting and somewhat erotic, watching Shane beat Mc Claskey like this. I felt myself begin to tingle as Shane beat Mc Claskey's face with a series of punches.

Get him baby. Get him good.

Shane was covered in sweat and his muscles flared with each swing. His hair was wet. His face, shoulders, legs, and chest - all soaked.

Something about a man covered in muscles and sweat really made me feel uneasy.

In a good way.

As Shane continued to beat on Mc Claskey, I began to feel myself getting wet.

Ding!

The crowd began to clap.

"Oh my God, that was exciting," I looked toward Ripp, smiling.

Ripp was rubbing his bald head and appeared to not even hear me. I turned to watch Shane and Kelsey. Kelsey was screaming at Shane and hitting his shoulders as he squirted water in his mouth.

My heart raced. People started chanting again.

I looked up at the steel structure above us and listened at the chants of the crowd.

Shame.....on!

Shame.....on!

Shame.....on!

Ding!

"Ripp, they're screaming for Shane!" I screeched as the bell rang.

The crowd continued to cheer. The cheers seemed to fuel Shane. Ripp and Kelsey both had said Shane heard everything as he fought. I squeezed the dog tags between my hands and hoped the cheers gave Shane courage. I turned toward Ripp, who stood shaking his fists in front of his chest.

As I turned back to the ring, Shane stood in the center as Mc Claskey approached. Shane pounded his gloves together.

"Here we go," Ripp screamed.

Do it again, baby. Do it again.

SHANE

If this prick thinks he has me figured out, he's dead wrong.

C'mon, you big son-of-a-bitch.

Mc Claskey approached and held his gloves close to his face. From what I could see in the first rounds, he didn't have much to counter my speed. Ripp, Kelsey, and Kace probably thought I was crazy in the first four rounds. I had to see what this big fucker was made of.

He's strong as fuck.

He's soft.

And he's slow.

I stepped in close and switched to southpaw.

Here's where I belong, big boy.

Coming at ya with…

This.

I swung a right hook into his ribs. As he exhaled what little breath might have been in his lungs, his face had a look of surprise his eyes couldn't hide.

I swung a left cross and caught the bottom of his jaw. As he turned to try to take me to the ropes, I stepped in close and clenched him, holding him still.

What, you big muscled up prick? You don't like fighting? You wanna wrestle?

He should have known I didn't like to push and shove. I let go and pushed him off.

I came here to fight.

I unleashed a series of punches to his mid-section - an unanswered barrage of hooks and jabs which would have dropped any previous fighter in my career.

I swung an uppercut, and barely missed his jaw.

Shame...

On.

Shame...

On.

The crowd cheered my name. I have never been a vain person, but an entire arena chanting my name was something I had never heard before. I hated to admit it, but I liked it. The chanting provided me a reason to show Mc Claskey why I chose boxing as a career.

He attempted to get me off of him with a right jab. An uppercut followed. Both were dodged without much effort. I stepped to his right, and swung a left hook into his ribs.

Oh shit, that felt like it cracked.

I've always said the eyes don't lie. And his didn't. He was hurt.

I knew what was next.

Lord. Prevent me from...

I swung a right-left hook combo into his torso.

Killing...

I threw a series of jabs to get him off balance.

This big bastard.

I threw my signature left hook into his ribs. He body twisted to his right, and both gloves came down for a fraction of a section. A fraction was all I needed.

I swung a right uppercut that connected directly with the bottom of his jaw. I followed with a left jab and landed solid on the front of his chin. His chin came down just a touch and his gloves dropped completely.

Everything went to slow motion for a moment. I heard the crowd cheering my name. I heard Kelsey pounding the mat, indicating the end of the round being only seconds away. And I heard, clear as day, Mike fucking Ripton scream.

You got this, Dekk!

A few times in my career, I have thrown a punch and regretted it. After they're thrown, it's impossible to stop, especially by someone with my speed and strength. The right cross I threw at Mc Claskey's temple was one of those punches. As soon as I threw it, I realized he was already unconscious. The punch connected on the left side of his temple. His head looked as if it was going to snap off of his neck.

He fell to the mat.

And he did not move.

I vaguely remember seeing the referee step in. I turned toward the crowd. Everyone was on their feet, cheering. I looked at Mc Claskey.

And he did not move.

The referee waved his hands.

And I realized I had gone the distance. Not in this fight, but in my career - and with Kace. The Heavyweight Championship of the world was next. If what I had read was correct, several million people should be watching Mc Claskey and I fight on Pay-Per-View. Without a doubt, I would be a household name overnight. The title fight would bring tens of millions of dollars, even if I lost the bout.

Mc Claskey moved his head.

Thank you Lord.

When they finally got Mc Claskey to his feet, I heard the announcer before I noticed all of the people gathered around me. And it sunk in.

I had actually won.

"…of the sixth round. By knockout. The winner, *Shane Shame on Dekkar.*"

As Kace stepped into the ring, my dog tags dangling from her clenched fist, I saw the look of pride in her eyes. As I stared at her I further realized - not only had I won the fight - *I had clearly won at the game of life.*

KACE

I've felt a wide range of emotion in my life, but I had never felt the emotion I felt when Shane's name was announced as the winner. I realized the potential upcoming Championship was a huge fight, but I really didn't care if Shane ever fought again. The fight he had won, to me, *was* the big fight.

"Shane, what's next for you? Where do you go from here?" the television reporter asked.

There were cameras and microphones everywhere. Shane had his arm around my shoulder, holding me close to his side. I clutched his dog tags tight in my hand. Ripp and Kelsey were both standing on Shane's left side. I realized what the announcer asked, and waited to hear how Shane would respond.

"Well, I'll have to consult with my manager, my trainer, my sparring partner," he paused and slapped Ripp with his taped hand.

"But, ultimately, I'll have to consult with my little woman," he pulled me close to his side and paused.

The microphone immediately moved in front of my face.

The reporter bent down, "So, ma'am, what's next for Shane Dekkar?"

A million thoughts ran through my head. Shane had made it this far, because he was a *fighter*. He fought not for money, not for fame, but to survive. He had told me he had demons, and the fighting *allowed* him to live. Out of the ring, Shane was the nicest man in the world and I couldn't imagine him being any other way. If what he said was right, the fighting permitted him to be who he was in his life. The fighting allowed him to clear his head of all of the things that potentially made other men evil.

To me, the answer was clear.

"I, uhhm. I'll say this. If Shane decides to challenge the Heavyweight Champion of the World, he has my blessing. But I'll leave the decision up to him," I whispered into the microphone.

Shane pulled me tighter to his side.

"So, what will it be Shane?" the reporter asked.

"That's all for tonight," Shane smiled.

"No more questions," Kelsey said as he stepped in front of Shane.

The reporter stepped aside and signed off to the camera with a few last words. Shane, Ripp, Kelsey and I walked to the ropes and ducked out of the ring and onto the floor. As we began to walk toward the aisle, Kelsey eagerly started to talk to Shane.

"So, Shane," he paused and turned to Shane.

"The championship fight. What are you thinking?" Kelsey asked.

Ripp and Kelsey both turned to Shane as we walked up the aisle.

"I'm not even thinking about that right now. I'm thinking about someone else's ass I got to beat," Shane said.

"Oh?" Kelsey asked.

"Kace's," Shane said sternly as he slowed his walking pace.

"For digging through the god damned trash," he chuckled as he stopped and turned to face me.

Slowly, he bent at the waist and waited for me to hang the dog tags around his neck.

KACE

When I was young, I dreamt of being swept off of my feet. I hoped one day there would be a boy that would love me, cherish me, and treat me with respect. As I got older, my visions of how that person would act, what he might look like, and what he would do to and for me changed. In recent years, thoughts of whether or not it would ever happen diminished.

Until now.

"A Kace Meadows? Is there a Kace Meadows who works here?" The delivery man asked as soon as he stepped through the door. His shirt said *F. T. C.*

I couldn't even speak. I opened my mouth and…

No words.

I raised my hand.

"Are you Kace Meadows?"

I tapped the desk once.

Shit, he doesn't know that code – one for yes, two for no.

I nodded eagerly and pointed at my chest.

"Okay, sign here," he said as he pointed at the screen of his electronic pad.

I signed quickly; still not convinced he had the right person or place.

I've never received flowers in my entire life.

Ever.

"Okay. Here you go. The card's right here," he said as he pointed to a little card holder in the center of the arrangement.

I eagerly nodded my head again.

"Have a nice day," he said as he turned toward the door.

I nodded my head again.

I pulled the card out of the holder and opened it.

KACE,
I WARNED YOU. I'M COMING FOR IT.
SHANE

Roses and baby's breath. I counted the roses. *Twenty four*.

Normally, when I went to the grocery store, I would admire roses at the floral department and take time to sneak a smell. I love flowers. I had never received any from anyone, and I had always wondered how it would make me feel to receive some.

Nothing compares.

Nothing.

I re-read the card. I smelled the flowers again.

Ahhhhh.

Shane was an angel, he really was. He took so many precautions to make sure he never did *anything* to hurt me. Everything he said, did, wanted, or liked was based on what he thought would make me happy. All from a man who was as unforgiving and brutal as he was in the boxing ring. Sometimes I couldn't comprehend how he could even be real.

"Kace, are you there?" Mr. Martin asked from the other side of the desk.

"I'm back here, Mr. Martin," I giggled.

"Oh, I couldn't see you behind the forest of flowers," he laughed.

"They're beautiful. I could smell them from my office. I didn't need anything - I just wanted to see them. Flowers are as beautiful as the loved one who sends them, Kace," he said as he bent down and smelled the roses.

"Enjoy them," he said as he turned away from the desk.

"Oh, I will," I responded excitedly.

I spent most of the morning smelling my flowers. Before lunch, I received a text message from Shane saying he was at the gym, and he would be busy for the remainder of the day. He said he would see me after work, and we would talk. I thanked him for the flowers, and he responded with a smiley face, which was out of character for him. He never texted, and he never sent smileys.

After lunch, I walked back to the office and sat at my desk. The entire office smelled like roses. I felt so proud to have the flowers. I sat and tried to think of what Shane may want to talk about, and eventually decided he probably wanted my approval to fight the championship fight.

The door opened again. A man in a uniform walked in. He had a sewn on patch on his blue uniform shirt. *Lofton Mini Cooper.* He leaned around the flowers and looked at me.

"Are you Kace Meadows?" he asked.

"Uhhm. Yes, I am. Can I help you?" I asked.

"Yes, it's about your car, can you come outside?" he asked as he turned and walked out the door.

How rude.

My heart sank. I had the same car since my senior year in high school. My Mazda Protégé. It had three hundred thousand miles on it, and it wasn't much, but it was all I had. If this rude man hit my car and it was damaged, I would have to take the bus to work.

"Mr. Martin, I have to go outside. Something's happened to my car. I'll be right back in," I yelled down the hallway.

"Okay, Kace. I'll answer the phones," he responded.

I stepped outside the office door and onto the sidewalk. The man stood beside the curb with another man who wore a shirt just like his.

"What happened to my car?" I asked.

"I'm not sure what you mean, ma'am. We're making a delivery. You're Kace Meadows?" he asked.

"Yes, I'm Kace Meadows, why?" I responded.

He held out a set of car keys.

"Delivery from Lofton Mini Cooper. From a Mr. Shane Dekkar. Just out of curiosity, how do you know Shane Dekkar?" he asked.

Confused, I looked at him and responded, "He's my boyfriend."

"Shane Dekkar, the boxer?" he asked.

I nodded my head slowly.

"Kip, this chic is Dekkar's girlfriend. The guy from here in town who fought on Pay-Per-View. *Shame on Dekkar,*" he said over his shoulder to the other man in the uniform.

"Holy shit. You think you could get us his autograph?" the other man asked.

Still confused, I shrugged my shoulders, "Uhhm. I don't know, maybe."

"Well, when you bring this in for service or warranty work, bring him with you," he said as he pointed toward the street.

"I don't understand what's going on," I responded.

"Oh, sorry," he said as he turned and dropped the keys into my hand.

I scrunched my brow and looked at the keys.

"From Mr. Dekkar. He bought you a new Mini Cooper," he said as he pointed to a new car sitting at the curb beside the other man.

My heart rose up into my throat. I turned and looked down the sidewalk in each direction.

"This isn't a joke?" I asked.

"No ma'am. We delivered it for him. Kip's taking me back to the dealer. Mr. Dekkar bought it from the sales department. We work in the service department. They just asked us to deliver it," he responded.

"You're not making a YouTube Video or something?" I asked.

"Nope," he said as he shook his head.

"This is mine?" I asked as I pushed the button on the keys.

The lights flashed and the horn honked.

"Yes ma'am."

I pushed the button again. The lights flashed and the horn honked again.

"Can I look inside?" I asked.

"Ma'am, you can do whatever you want. It's *your* car. Bring Mr. Dekkar out to see us if you can. You ready Kip?" he turned to ask the other man.

I pushed the button on the keys again. I looked at the outside of the car, which was a beautiful silver color. I opened the door. I pushed on the seat with my hand. *Oh God, black leather interior.* The car smelled like brand new. *It was brand new.*

Squeeeeeeee!

I ran into the office and sat at my desk. It was simply too much to comprehend. I was living in a dream. A real life dream. I sat and wondered if someone was going to come take the car later and say it was all a big joke. I held the key in the air and pushed the button.

Beep!

I pushed it again.

Beep!

I knew Shane was training, and I didn't want to disturb him, but I felt I had to say something. I was far too excited to keep my mouth shut. I picked up my phone and sent him a text message.

Shane: OMG! Someone brought me a car. Do you know anything about this?

I picked up my desk phone and pushed the button to connect me to Mr. Martin's desk.

"What is it, Kace?" he asked.

"Someone brought me a new car, Mr. Martin. I just wanted to tell you," I squealed.

"What do you mean, Kace?" he asked, his voice filled with surprise.

"That's what I said when they brought it. Uhhm. *Shane.* He bought me a car and had the boys from the dealership deliver it. It's silver and so cute. I just thought I'd tell you," I giggled.

"I'll be up in a minute," he chuckled.

Immediately, I heard Mr. Martin walking down the hallway toward my desk. As he approached my desk, he leaned over and smelled the roses.

"I can't smell those enough, Kace. A bouquet of roses puts my mind at ease. Let's have a look at the car, shall we?" he said as he held his hand out.

I dropped my keys in his hand, stood up from my seat at the desk and straightened the wrinkles from my skirt. As I stepped around the desk, the aroma from the flowers made me smile. As my body cleared the edge of the desk, Mr. Martin held out his free hand. As we walked outside together, he held my hand in his.

"A new car. That's' quite a gift," he said as he held the office door open.

"He's quite a guy, Mr. Martin," I smiled as I looked up at him.

He pushed the button on the keys.

Beep!

He turned and looked toward the sound of the horn and pushed the key button again.

Beep!

"*Oh my.* A Mini Cooper. That's a fabulous choice on his part, Kace. This will be great car. These things have been the car of choice in Europe for decades and decades, and for good reason. They have great gas mileage, outstanding performance and they're a pleasure to drive. It's gorgeous, Kace. I'm happy for you," he said as he looked in the window of the car.

"Now this is Shane, the boxer?" he asked as he turned and handed me the keys.

I nodded my head, "Yes sir."

"He's perceptive, isn't he?" he asked as he turned to face the entrance to the office.

"How so?" I asked.

"He recognizes you as being valuable. As being beautiful. As being, well," he paused and raised his hand to his chin.

"Special. He sees you as special. And he's doing his best to tell you.

Or, shall I say, *show* you how he feels," he said as he held the door open for me.

"I suppose so, I really like him," I responded as I walked through the door.

"A little advice?" he turned my direction and smiled.

"Okay," I responded.

"Starting right now, don't ever be anyone but *you*. And be one hundred percent honest with him regarding your wants, desires, and hopes. Tell him what it is that you expect and want in the relationship. Don't sacrifice what *you* want for the sake or thought of making him happy. Make him understand what it is that's important to you from the start. If you don't, you'll forever regret what it is you're giving up – what it is that you're *not* receiving. If you tell him now, you'll give him the chance to discuss it, consider it, or ultimately – provide it," he adjusted his neck tie, smiled, and looked down at his shoes.

He seemed to become sad.

"For ten years of marriage, Mrs. Martin didn't bake sweets because she felt she didn't want to tempt me to eat unhealthy foods. For ten years, I snuck to the diner alone and ate a slice of pie. I ate a different type of pie every time I went. I love pie, by the way," he paused and smiled.

"I lived with ten years of guilt for sneaking out and eating the pie alone. She lived with ten years of misery for giving up something she truly loved – baking pastries and sweets. Had we only discussed it in the beginning, those ten years would have been so much better for us both. It might sound silly or simple, but that's just an example," he adjusted his tie and offered another smile.

"Thank you, Mr. Martin," I smiled, "I'll do that."

As he walked down the hall to his office, I went back to my desk and made a list.

Of what was important to *me* in a relationship.

SHANE

Kace had become the most important thing in my life. In many respects, Kace had *become* my life. For me to admit Kace's importance was simple and second nature. Two years ago, I suspect it would have been impossible for me to admit. Now, however, I didn't hesitate. Now that I had had Kace in my life, to imagine *not* having her made me feel extremely uneasy.

I wasn't simply attracted to Kace. I felt as if I *needed* her. Merely having her accompany me in life provided me with a feeling of completion. Similar, I suppose, to concluding a long journey.

Kace made me stop. Stop wanting. Stop wondering. Stop looking. Stop thinking. Stop running.

And begin.

Living, breathing, and being.

I didn't feel an attraction to her because she'd been in an abusive relationship. I didn't feel as if I had rescued her either. I truly believed I opened her eyes and provided her with ideas of what her options were. I loved Kace because she was genuine. I loved Kace because she was a beautiful person.

I loved Kace because she was Kace.

"A list, huh?" I chuckled as I pulled a bottle of water from the refrigerator.

"I'm serious. I brought it home with me. I put a lot of thought into it," she paused and waited at the end of the kitchen countertop.

"I wasn't laughing at your list, babe. I was laughing because you're so fucking adorable. You're different than any other girl I've ever known. At least after leaving Buster, you aren't afraid to say what you think. I like it. I like *you*," I said as I walked her direction.

"Well, you want to go over it?" she asked as she pulled a folded sheet of yellow paper from her purse.

"Absolutely, let's go in the living room," I said as I walked past her.

She kicked her heels off onto the kitchen floor and ran past me as I walked to the couch. She bounced into the chair on the opposite side of the couch and unfolded the sheet of paper.

"You don't want to sit together?" I asked as I sat down on the couch, patting the cushion beside me with my hand.

"Nope. I want to sit here and watch you while we talk," she bounced excitedly in the cushion as she spoke.

"Okay, let's get to it," I responded as I took a sip of water from the bottle.

"Okay, here's what I would want to be in a perfect relationship with you. I want to know if these things are okay with you, not okay, or something we could discuss. Some are really important, and some not as much. I decided we need to get this out of the way," she flipped her hair over her shoulders and stretched the wrinkles from the paper.

"What if I take exception to something?" I asked, more jokingly than serious.

"Well, depending on what it is, we'll address it at the time, but be honest," she nodded her head sharply as she finished the sentence.

"Okay."

"Promise?" she turned her head slightly and smiled.

"Totally," I responded.

"Okay, here we go," she paused.

"I like to cook. You and Ripp like to eat out. I want to cook at least five meals a week at home, and I want you to eat them. You don't have to like them, but no throwing food at me, screaming at me about what I cook, and no telling me I'm stupid for cooking something you don't like. I know you want to eat healthy food, and I will take it into consideration. I like healthy too. Yes or no," she looked up from the paper.

"Is that how we're going to do this? Yes or no?" I asked as I placed the water on the end table beside the couch.

She tapped her hand once on the arm of the couch.

I shook my head and smiled.

This woman makes me fucking happy.

"Yes," I said.

"Okay. Next one. I want to wash my own car. I don't want you washing it. You can drive it or whatever, because we're a couple. But I want to wash it," she looked up and into my eyes as she finished reading.

"Yes," I grinned.

She smiled and looked down at the paper, "Okay, next. I want to get a Goodreads account, Facebook, and maybe some other things on the internet. I think this will help me become more social. Oh, and I want more friends - more than Liv from the coffee shop. I want *real* friends," as she looked up from the paper her face began to look worried.

"Yes," I responded sharply.

She bounced in her chair and pulled excitedly on each side of the wrinkled paper to straighten the wrinkles.

"Okay. Next. I'm almost done," she paused.

"I know I don't *have* to say this, but I *need* to. It's important," she looked up from the paper and waited.

"Okay?" I responded.

Without looking down at the paper, she continued, "If you ever lay a hand on me. Slap me, hit me, grab me, push me, *anything*. I'm gone. I'll leave you and *never* come back."

She looked as if she was going to start crying.

"Kace, I'll never lay a hand on you. Ever. I promise," I responded.

I realized it was a huge step for her to even mention this. It was her way of taking a stance against what had already happened to her. She wiped her face as one single tear ran down her cheek with the back of her hand and sniffed.

"Okay. I just had to say it," she said softly.

She looked down at the paper. "Last thing," she folded the paper and stood up.

I stood up.

"No, you sit. I'll be right back," she said as she took off in a dead run for the kitchen.

I turned and looked over my shoulder as she reached into her purse and pulled out her Kindle. She ran back to the chair and plopped down, bouncing in her seat as she turned on the device.

"Let me finish," she said as she stared at the screen of the Kindle.

"Kace you need to start first," I responded.

"I know. I'm just saying, this is a long one," she said as she flipped her finger across the screen of the Kindle.

"Okay," I responded as I picked up my bottle of water from the end table.

"You're not going to hurt me emotionally from sex. You're too cautious, too careful, and you never even talk during sex. I'm not as fragile as you think. I've spent ten years getting *fucked over*, and not getting *fucked.* I want you to fuck me sometimes. And sometimes we can make love. But I never want you to worry about fucking me and harming me emotionally. This is what I want," she looked up from the screen of her Kindle as she finished talking.

"Oh. Wow, okay. Well, what do you mean, specifically? Regarding fucking?" I asked, shocked this was her last question.

She jumped up from her seat and squeaked as she did. She handed me her Kindle and ran quickly back to her seat.

"Look at the screen. See the number at the bottom? 24%? Start there and read about five pages," she said as she bounced up and down in her seat.

I looked down at the Kindle and began reading.

"Just flip your finger across the screen to turn the page," she said.

I nodded as I read.

I finished the five pages.

Wow.

"Is that it?" I asked as I looked up from the Kindle.

"Nope," she said excitedly.

Instantly, she jumped up, ran toward me and snatched the Kindle from my grasp. Almost frantically, she pushed and flipped her finger across the screen. She smiled and handed it back to me.

"Those two and a half pages. From the top of where it is," she smiled and pranced back to her perch.

As she sat down, she pressed the wrinkles from her skirt. I read the two and a half pages, placed the Kindle down beside me, and took a slow drink of water from my bottle.

"Yes," I said.

She emitted a loud squeal and jumped from her seat, her arms outstretched.

"Sit down, Kace," I said sternly as I stood up.

She frowned and sat down in her seat. She looked up at me with a puzzled look as I slowly approached her.

"Give me your hand," I said as I held my hand out toward her lap.

She raised her hand to mine, grasped my fingers in hers, and rose from her seat as I lifted her hand in mine.

"What…" she began to ask as I pulled her up from her seat.

"Not a word," I said as I began to walk toward the spare bedroom.

As we approached the weight bench, I lifted her hand over her head and spun her in a half-circle. As she faced me, I released her hand. Slowly, I reached up and held her face in my hands. I leaned forward and kissed her deeply. As we kissed she began to moan. I reached under her skirt as we kissed and pulled her panties down to mid-thigh. I continued to kiss her and lifted my foot to the height of her thigh and pushed her panties to the floor.

I pulled my lips from hers and turned her head to the side.

I leaned toward her ear and whispered heavily, "Kace, there's only one rule. Always. One for yes, twice for no. That's the only rule, okay?"

She tapped my shoulder once as she exhaled a light sigh. I bit the bottom of her earlobe sharply and turned her head to face me. As soon as she made eye contact, I pressed my lips to hers. As we kissed I lifted her from the floor and placed her down on the weight bench. On her back, with her legs on each side of the bench, I continued to kiss her deeply, biting her lips harshly each time our mouths parted.

I reached down and pulled the leg extension attachment upward.

"Put your feet here," I said as I lifted her heels up toward the extension.

Without argument or explanation, she complied. In this position, it was similar to being in the stirrups in a doctor's office for an examination. I unzipped her skirt and removed it, tossing it on the spare bed.

"Not a word, Kace," I reminded her, "Now close your eyes. Don't open them."

She closed her eyes, lifted her head from the bench, and placed her hands behind her head. As she did, I pressed her knees apart and buried my face between her legs. As I began to lick her soaking wet pussy, she moaned loudly.

I moaned as I licked and fingered her pussy, paying special attention to her swollen clit. She continued to groan as I slid my finger in and out of her soaking wet pussy and flicked my tongue across her clit. As I slid my finger in and out of her pussy, her breathing became short and choppy. I felt her pussy walls begin to contract against my finger.

"Shane…" she moaned.

As my finger slid in and out, I continued to lick and suck her clit.

"Shane. Oh…God," she whispered. Her hands slipped from behind her head and she grabbed the sides of the weight bench.

With my free hand, I unbuckled my belt and unzipped my jeans.

"Holy….fuck," she groaned as she began to reach climax.

She raised her butt from the bench and pressed her pussy tight to my mouth. As she dropped her ass back to the bench, she exhaled and opened her eyes.

"Oh my God," she whispered.

I stood and kicked my jeans to the side. I pulled my shirt off and tossed it beside the jeans.I stood naked in front of her and smiled as I looked down. As she began to sit up on the bench, I grabbed my cock and started stroking it.

"Oh God," she moaned as she watched me.

"Watch me, Kace. Watch me stroke it," I said.

I began stroking it faster, and leaned back as I began to moan. I closed my eyes and stroked my cock as I thought of Kace and her sexual wishes.

"Oh, God, this feels good. And, just so you know, I fucking love licking your sweet little pussy Kace," I said as I leaned forward and opened my eyes.

She was lying on the weight bench with her legs spread She had two fingers in her pussy, fingering it like she was working against the clock. Her eyes were fixed on my stiff cock. She tilted her head back and closed her eyes as she began to cum.

"Oh God, Shane. Oh God," she stopped speaking as her breathing became short inhaled breaths followed by a sharp exhale.

"Holy…"

She opened her eyes and looked up as she stopped fingering her pussy. Slowly, she exhaled a breath and shook her head.

"Fuck," she pulled her fingers from her pussy and opened her mouth.

She smiled and raised her hand to her face. Slowly, she slid her fingers in her mouth, sucking and licking each of them individually. Overwhelmed, I stepped onto the weight bench and stood.

"Move your feet to the floor," I said in somewhat of a demanding tone.

Immediately, she dropped her feet from the leg extensions and placed her feet on the floor.

"Put your hands up in the butterfly attachments," I said.

She reached to either side of her head and grasped the attachments. Now sitting on the end of the bench, naked except for her sleeveless shirt, her feet were on the floor and her hands rested at each side of her head.

"Don't move," I said as stepped onto the bench.

I walked along the weight bench toward her.

"Open your mouth," I whispered as I stood directly in front of her face.

As soon as she opened her mouth, I placed my hands around her head, gripping it tightly. I slowly and steadily forced my cock into her mouth. Her eyes widened as the tip of my cock bumped into the back of her throat. I held my cock in place and massaged her head with my fingers.

"I like my cock in your throat, Kace. I like it there. I'm glad you like wild, crazy rough sex. I like it too," I said as I slowly pulled my cock from her mouth.

As soon as the tip cleared her lips, she gasped for breath. As she took a breath she reached for my thighs.

"No. Put your hands back up there, on the attachments," I demanded.

She grasped the attachments in her hands and took another breath. As she looked up at me, I slowly leaned forward, forcing my cock into her mouth. I grasped the sides of her head, and began to slowly fuck her mouth.

As my cock slid in and out of her mouth, I made certain to push hard enough to press into her throat with each stroke in. I stopped with the tip against her throat, and took a deep breath.

"You like that, babe?" I said as I exhaled.

She tapped the attachment once and blinked her eyes.

I pulled my cock from her mouth. Saliva dripped from her lips as my cock cleared her mouth. I reached down and wiped her mouth as I held out my hand.

"Grab my hand, babe," I said as I held my hand in front of her.

"Babe, I'm soaked," she said as she stood up, her feet on either side of the bench.

As she stood, I looked down at the bench where she was lying. There was a wet spot the size of a grapefruit where her pussy was.

"That's the idea, Kace. Soaked is good," I explained as I jumped down from the bench.

I led her to the bed and softly pushed her down on her back.

"You feeling flexible?" I asked.

"I think so," she responded.

"Okay, pull your knees to your chest. I'm going to fuck you ragged," I said.

"Uhhm," she started to respond.

"Pull them up there, Kace," I said as I climbed onto the bed.

She reached behind her knees and locked her fingers together. As she pulled her knees to her chest, I pressed my hips against her calves, forcing her feet against her ass, and her pussy straight up in the air.

Immediately I forced my entire cock inside of her soaked pussy. She gasped for air as soon as I began to push myself into her.

"Hold those legs," I demanded.

I began to use every ounce of energy I had to fuck her. My stamina was tremendous, and I wanted to use this opportunity to prove a point. I wanted this to be an orgasm she remembered for some time. I took a breath and began forcefully fucking her as fast and as hard as I could.

About a minute and a half into it, she began to scream.

"Holy….shit….Shane," she breathed as she opened her eyes.

"I'm…"

"Oh my God…"

"I want it dripping off my balls, Kace," I growled.

"Ahhhhhhhhhh Fuccccckkkkkk," she groaned as her eyes widened and then closed again.

She exhaled as I slowed my pace.

"Are you…"

"Going to…"

"Finish?" she muttered.

"Oh, hell no. I can do this all night," I bragged as I continued to pound my cock in and out of her.

"Get ready," I said.

She pulled her knees close to her chest as I began increasing my pace. I shoved my cock inside of her as far as I could, and as fast as possible.

Considering my typical forms of physical conditioning, fucking wasn't a form of exercise - it was a form of *relaxation*. I continued to pound myself into her wet pussy as she began to groan.

I looked down and watched as my cock disappeared repeatedly onto her swollen pussy.

"I'm gonna…" she sighed.

"Cum," she let go of her legs and covered her eyes.

I pressed against her knees with my torso, holding them to her chest. I continued to pound myself in and out of her pussy steadily.

"Ohhhhh…..myyyyyy…..God," she moved her hands and opened her eyes.

She raised her hands in the air and waved them as if she wanted to stop. I moved my face to beside her ear, resting my forehead on the pillow.

"Give me a minute, Kace," I breathed into her ear.

I began to fuck her without reservation, knowing this would be a huge orgasm for her. Her body, from the force of me fucking her, began to inch closer and closer to the headboard. As I continued to fuck her, she began to breathe heavily. Her head started to bounce onto the wall with each stroke.

Bam!

Bam!

Bam!

I continued to shove my cock into her as deep as possible and as rapid of a pace as I could deliver. I lowered my face to her ear again.

"You like this, Kace?" I whispered as I pounded her soaking wet pussy.

No response, only breathing.

"Holy fuck!" she screamed as her pussy contracted.

I pounded away.

"Shane!" she screamed as her body noticeably shook.

I reached down and grabbed one butt cheek and spread her pussy wider, forcing myself in as far as I could. I held my cock as deep as possible as she had orgasm after orgasm.

"Ohhhhhh!" she began waving her arms frantically as she screamed.

She opened her eyes and pressed her hands against my chest.

"Don't…Stop…Get off!" she demanded.

"What's wrong?" I asked, my face covered in a huge smile.

"Shhhhh," she sighed.

"Kace?" I asked.

She raised her hand in the air between us.

I looked at her face and smiled. Her eyes closed, covered in sweat, and attempting to recover from a humongous orgasm, her entire body quivered.

"Kace?" I asked, knowing it would irritate her.

She raised her hand again, "Shut up, Shane. Gimme a minute."

I rolled from the bed and walked naked to my bedroom. Slowly and quietly, I walked back into the room.

I lowered myself onto the bed, and softly pressed myself against her.

"You okay now?" I asked.

"Better," she smiled, her eyes still closed.

"What happened?" I asked.

"You know what happened. Death by orgasm," she held her fingers in the air, her thumb and forefinger a hair apart.

"That close," she said, her eyes still closed.

I smiled.

"Take your time, babe. I love you," I said softly as I kissed her stomach.

"I love you," she said, still relaxing with her eyes closed.

"Remember what I said about needing to talk to you?" I asked.

"Uh huh," she responded.

"Well, I have a simple question for you Kace. Well, I guess it's a statement and a question," I said.

She opened her eyes.

"Just like you said earlier, let me finish, okay?" I asked.

She nodded.

"My father Kace. He abused my mother. I had repressed the memory

261

for my entire life. That day when we opened the chest, I had a mental breakdown. My mind brought all of the memories back, and I shut down. The second day, I went to a psychiatrist. He brought up a lot of points about my childhood. We don't need to talk about all of them now, but I'll tell you a few," I took a deep breath and kissed her stomach again.

"My father used to beat my mother, and the only place I had to hide was in my room. I hid under a blanket that I thought was special. I thought it had protective powers. I thought if I hid under it, he wouldn't beat me, and that he was also not really beating my mother. It's taken me a month to realize some of these things," I took another shallow breath and kissed her stomach.

"I hide in my hoodie as a result of my childhood. I find comfort there. It's sad, but I know now it's why I wear it. I'm not ready to stop wearing it Kace, but I think I'm getting better," I kissed her stomach again as she wiped tears from her eyes.

"I hated my father for a while after going to the psychiatrist. But that speech you gave at the fight…well, it made all too much sense. I already felt that way, but you saying it made it sink in. I suppose my father was sick about my mother leaving. And his way of clearing his head was to fight the only way he knew – as a US Marine in a war that he couldn't win. He died fighting. In a sense, he died fighting so he didn't have to beat another woman. At least that's what I'm thinking," I paused and took another breath as I started to fill with emotion.

I got this.

"My grandfather did the same thing. I'm sure of it. He beat my grandmother until she left. I don't remember it, *not really*. But I am starting to. Generations of abuse creates generations of abusers. The chain has to be broken, and rebuilt. It can't merely be broken and left alone, or it's all for nothing," I explained.

With both hands and without talking, she wiped the tears from her eyes. It was all I could do to see her cry. I attempted to maintain my composure as I finished speaking.

I was almost done.

I took another breath.

"Now, the question," I exhaled.

KACE

I was an emotional mess. I wasn't ready for all of this talk. Shane had me on cloud nine, and now this talk was so sad. I felt so sorry for him, for his father, and for his grandfather. I felt sorry for their wives.

Basically, they were me.

We were the same.

Shane is a good man. I know he couldn't control his father, especially not as a child. After his explanation, his desire to fight made a lot more sense. He was fighting against everything that he hated. He was fighting to make everything make sense.

He was fighting for me and those like me.

"So, the chain. It's gotta be broken and rebuilt," he said as he lifted his lips from my stomach.

"People in an abusive relationship have children. The girls grow up and get beaten. The boys grow up and beat women. From time to time, a girl or boy is born who is different. I'm that boy. But for me Kace, for me - I need to *fix* this. I need to do something to fix it," he paused and looked into my eyes.

"*To fix me,*" he breathed.

He rubbed his face with his hand and took a breath.

"This is where you come in," he smiled.

"Kace. Someday I want to. Not right now, but someday. I want to have children with you. I want that. I want to raise children the right way. I want to raise them in a house with a yard and a swing set and everything else kids need. I want to be there every day and provide them with the answer to every question they can muster," he paused and took a breath.

His eyes were filled with tears, but none leaked out.

I couldn't take it any longer. I sat up and wrapped my arms around him. I loved Shane with every morsel of my existence. No one, at any time or place, has ever loved or respected a man as much as I loved and respected Shane Dekkar.

I held him a close as I could and smashed my body against his.

My flowers.

My car.

One day he wants kids

My chin resting on his shoulder, I held my arms around his waist. He stared at the wall, resting his chin on his clenched fists. I had felt so much emotion in the last few hours, it seemed as if I was going to have a nervous breakdown. I needed to be strong for Shane. It wasn't very often he needed me to hold him up, but when he did, I needed to be strong.

"Which brings us to the question," he said.

I raised my chin from his shoulder.

He took a deep breath.

I can't take any more.

Please no more.

"Kace," he barely got my name out of his mouth without losing composure.

"Kace, I need to…" he turned his head to the side and licked his dry lips.

"Know something," he said as he moved his head from his hands.

He opened his clenched fist and reached into his palm with his other hand.

"Would you consider marrying me?" he asked as he removed a diamond ring from his palm.

As he held the ring up, I burst into tears and grabbed his shoulders again. I sobbed and shook as I held him in my arms.

My entire life, since about thirteen, all I ever wanted was to get married and have children. To be able to do it with Shane would make me the happiest woman on earth. Incapable of comprehending the emotions I was feeling, I sobbed and held him in my arms.

"Kace?" he asked, holding the ring over his shoulder in front of my face.

I looked up at the diamond ring.

Holy. Mother. Of. God.

I wanted the ring more than anything. I wanted to be his wife.

"Kace? Will you marry me?" he asked, his voice shaking.

The ring shook in his hand.

I held him in my arms, sobbing, and opened my mouth.

No words.

"Kace?" he asked softly.

"Kace, will you?"

Tears dripped off of my chin onto his back. I needed to answer him. Inside my head, I said *yes*, but my mouth wouldn't work. I lowered my hands and massaged my tears into his back.

I opened my mouth.

Nothing.

"Kace? Babe?" he asked nervously.

And I did the only thing I knew to do.

I raised my hand and tapped him on his back.

Once.

For yes.

CPSIA information can be obtained
at www.ICGtesting.com
Printed in the USA
LVHW090113050121
675744LV00022B/65